TOM THOMSON'S LAST PADDLE

TOM THOMSON'S LAST PADDLE

A Dani and Caitlin Mystery

Larry McCloskey

An imprint of
Beach Holme Publishing
Vancouver

First Edition

This book is published by Beach Holme Publishing, 226–2040 West 12th Avenue, Vancouver, B.C. V6J 2G2. *www.beachholme.bc.ca*. This is a Sandcastle Book.

The publisher gratefully acknowledges the financial support of the Canada Council for the Arts and of the British Columbia Arts Council. The publisher also acknowledges the financial assistance received from the Government of Canada through the Book Publishing Industry Development Program (BPIDP) for its publishing activities.

Editor: John Burns
Production and Design: Jen Hamilton
Cover Art: Julia Bell
Author Photograph: Cara Lipsett
Map: Dale Taylor

Printed and bound in Canada by AGMV Marquis Imprimeur

National Library of Canada Cataloguing in Publication Data

McCloskey, Larry.
Tom Thomson's last paddle

"A Sandcastle book."
ISBN 0-88878-430-9

1. Thomson, Tom, 1877-1917—Juvenile fiction. I. Title.
PS8575.C635T65 2002 jC813'.6 C2002-910161-1
PZ7.M13355To 2002

To my mom: first Enie O'Neill from Navan,
then Irene McCloskey from Ottawa,
now just Enie from heaven.

ACKNOWLEDGEMENTS

I would like to thank the following for their support in the writing of this book: Cara, Kristen, Shannon, Caitlin, Dale, Rick, Donna, Pat, Diane, Isobell, Mary, Louise, Claudia, and Dani.

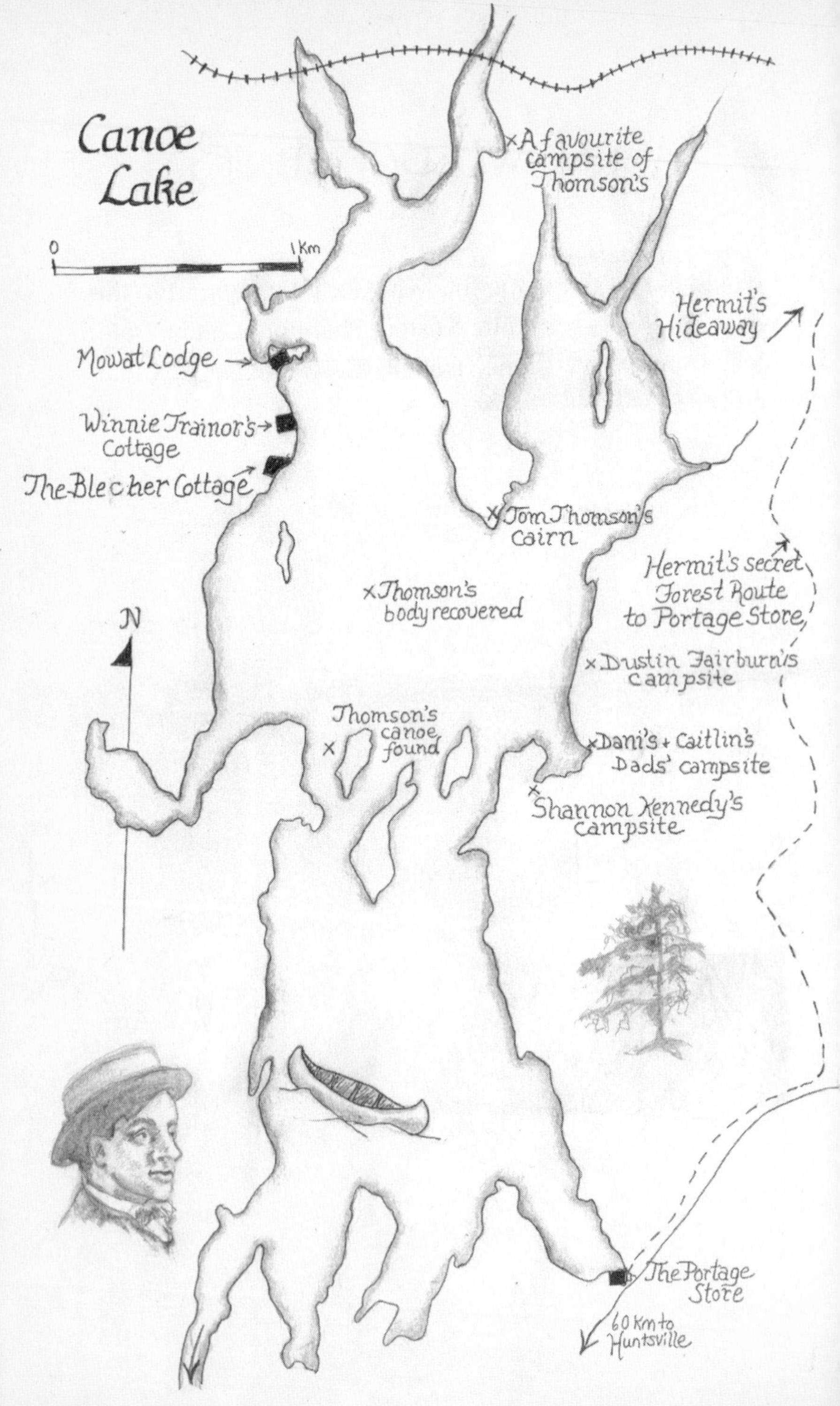

Canoe Lake
0
1 Km
Mowat Lodge
Winnie Trainor's Cottage
The Blecher Cottage
N
A favourite campsite of Thomson's
Hermit's Hideaway
Tom Thomson's Cairn
Hermit's secret Forest Route to Portage Store
Thomson's body recovered
Dustin Fairburn's campsite
Thomson's canoe found
Dani's + Caitlin's Dads' campsite
Shannon Kennedy's campsite
The Portage Store
60 Km to Huntsville

1
Famous Last Words

"I'm bored," Dani sighed.

"What took you so long?" Caitlin asked. "I've been bored ever since these trees started. I mean, have you ever seen so many trees? Trees, and trees, and trees—it's enough to drive a person insane. Trees to the left, trees to the right. Bored? Of course, you're bored."

"You should never be bored in this life," Dani's dad announced in a deep voice from the front of the van.

"It comes with the territory of being twelve-year-olds, John," Caitlin's dad interjected.

John ignored his friend. "Why, look at the magnificence of the landscape, the history of the area." Gripping the wheel tightly and Ping-Ponging his head repeatedly to make eye contact with the girls in the back seat, he seemed to be bouncing with the excitement of personally introducing two preteens to Mother Nature.

Dani and Caitlin exchanged glances. They had something

other than nature in mind for this trip with their fathers.

"Did you know that in two months' time," John continued, "along this very Ottawa Valley, we'll be able to experience the most dramatic fall colours in the entire world? Think of that the next time you get bored. Why—"

"Sure, Dad. But remember, you promised us a real juicy mystery," Dani interrupted, winking at her friend beside her. "That's the reason we agreed to come on this nature tour of Algonquin Park. We want to find out about this Tom Thomson guy 'cause you said something about him being a big mystery. Isn't that right, Caitlin?"

"Oh, absolutely. Absolutely."

This wasn't, strictly speaking, true. Dani and Caitlin had been working on a plan since winter to get their dads to take them camping in Algonquin—they thought they might prefer the call of the wild to their bossy older sisters, the heat of the city, and stupid boys with nothing better to do than sit around with garden hoses ready to soak them at every turn. Nature to the girls meant a fun week convincing their pliable dads of marshmallowy fine dining and daily trips into the visitor centre for gelato and magazines. It would be the perfect holiday.

The trick was to divert attention from their scheme and make it seem as if it was their dads' idea. John and Bob hadn't known each other very well, and neither was particularly skilled at camping. So the girls puzzled and puzzled all through the spring until they came up with the perfect reason for their dads to become friends: running! Both men were self-described "skinny, angst-ridden, obsessive Irish runner types." Whenever they referred to themselves as such, they would laugh long and loud, even though it wasn't funny the first time. Still, it got the job done. The men became good friends, took the bait about camping, and soon surprised the girls with their brilliant idea about camping in Algonquin Park.

But while the girls thought the camping trip was about mystery and gelato, the dads seriously seemed to think they were going to Algonquin Park to discover nature, and something about surviving in it. What fun could there be in that?

"We'll get to the juicy part in a minute, Dani, but first you have to know something about one of Canada's foremost landscape painters," Dani's father announced, perched so far forward in the driver's seat he was mostly addressing the windshield wipers. "And he just happens to be closely associated with the place where we're camping—Canoe Lake."

John pretended not to hear the complaints from the girls in the back seat. Still, for all their harmonious groaning, Dani and Caitlin were not particularly alike. Dani's eyes were green and Caitlin's were blue. Dani's denim overalls and greasy brown pigtails were her constant companions, while Caitlin's many outfits and blond French braids were perfectly styled and always in fashion. Dani loved mysteries and misadventure, while Caitlin preferred adventure, and it was a mystery to her why Dani seemed to be drawn to double trouble. The girls were best friends.

"Now," John continued, "everyone assumes Canoe Lake was named by Tom Thomson, but it was actually named by two explorers—Alexander Murray and later David Thompson, spelled with a *p*. Both of these men made split-cedar canoes in the surrounding area in the mid-1800s."

Dani's dad continued his rambling history as he glanced across at Bob, who was nodding with interest, and to the girls in the back of the van, just to be sure they were listening. With each look away from the road, Bob grimaced and nodded extra hard just to make certain his friend knew he was listening. Sitting between the two inattentive twelve-year-olds, Nikki, Dani's beagle, snorted, snored, and drooled. A painter might have been tempted to call this portrait of canine contentment a natural sleepscape.

"Dani, I warn you. I don't have your mother's ability to remove bubble gum from hair," John said, swivelling his head with the force of a lawn sprinkler in time to catch Dani's latest attempt at the world bubble-blowing record.

"Now, of course, you've probably seen some of Thomson's better-known paintings—*The West Wind*, *Northern River*..."

"And *The Jack Pine*," Bob added from the passenger seat.

"Yes, *The Jack Pine*, definitely," Dani's dad agreed. "During the First World War, no one painted quite like him. He was an innovator who influenced the Group of Seven. In fact, *The Canadian Encyclopedia* described his style as a 'smash and stab of passion flying before thought.' What's more, he was an outdoorsman, a naturalist, a park guide, a skilled canoeist..."

Dani's latest giant bubble smacked as she flipped through a book and periodically vocalized a lethargic "Uh-huh." Meanwhile Caitlin, steeped in the sunshine coming through the van's windows on this humid August morning, struggled to keep her eyes open.

John lifted an eyebrow with annoyance. "Oh, I'm being boring, I guess."

Dani gathered her gum and poised for another attempt as Caitlin thrust her head upward, alert but not particularly aware. "Oh, no, sir, we were following your story."

Looking at her friend, Dani placed a hand over one side of her mouth and whispered, "Sucker."

Caitlin continued to incriminate herself in a groggy, slurred voice. "Camping and painting…7-Eleven, yes, very interesting."

John's second eyebrow climbed next to its neighbour. "Yes, well, it seems Thomson inexplicably turned to canvas after a successful career painting all the 7-Eleven stores. Of course, there were only a couple dozen in the chain around the First World War."

Dani's gum bubble popped again, this time covering much of her nose. "Darn, I was so close." As she struggled to gather the remnants of her deflated masterpiece, she added matter-of-factly, "Sorry, Dad, but where exactly is the mystery here?"

John sighed and rolled his eyes at Bob, who rolled his eyes back at John.

"And another thing," Dani added, picking gum off her nose, "how come his parents called him Tom? Didn't they remember their own last name? And doesn't Thomson mean son of Tom? So was his dad's last name Thomson, too?"

Nothing came from the front seat but sighs. Caitlin tried to seem alert so Dani's dad wouldn't be insulted. But her eyes were very, very heavy. The sunlight was so warm and comforting, and the movement of the car lulled her into seductive sleep. With thoughts of down-filled comforters, Caitlin let her head sink, her face moulded to the car window as a small stream of drool seeped from her misshapen mouth. From deep, deep within the well of her mind a more conscious and alert Caitlin struggled to ascend the slippery wall and rouse the dozy girl creating the pool of liquid on the window. Several times she managed to climb to the top, peer out, and catch fragments of what Dani's dad was saying, but each time she slipped back down and landed in that comfortable place. Looking up at the well opening, she vaguely wondered why she even struggled, why she didn't just lie back and enjoy the tingling sensation of sleep. And then that rambling voice began again…

"Goes off on his own into the wilderness, paints these national treasures…and I'm talking about over three hundred sketches and at least twenty-four canvases in just three and a half years…sells some for next to nothing or gives them away…a few people in the know start to understand he's a really good painter, especially after the Ontario government pays $250 for a single painting, *Northern Lake*, quite a sum for a relative unknown at the time.

"This begins to establish his reputation—or notoriety, to some—but to the residents of Canoe Lake, where he spends most of his time from early spring until late fall, he's just Tom Thomson, keen fisherman, skilled outdoorsman, expert canoeist, and all-round regular guy. Kind of a loner, nice guy, liked by most people. Even has a girlfriend among the summer residents of Canoe Lake, an otherwise resident of Huntsville.

"Well, actually it's never really known just what the nature of the relationship is. In fact, it's never exactly clear what happened during the days and hours leading up to his unexpected death on July 8, 1917. The whole saga of Thomson's life and death at Canoe Lake remains to this day a living mystery, with the cloud of murder always hanging over the case, a sort of stormy silence that won't go away. Why, even now—"

Something caught Dani's attention as she carefully spread her gum across her teeth. Something caught Caitlin's attention from the depths of the down-filled well where she lay blissfully imprisoned by a thousand pillows.

"Mystery?" Dani asked with sudden excitement.

"Murder?" Caitlin questioned with a slight slur from that pesky saliva that left distortions of her face on the window.

The dads looked at each other, then quickly into the back seat.

"Dad, could you please tell us more about this mystery? And, by the way, we can hear fine when you're looking at the road."

"And don't forget about the murder, please, sir," a wide-awake Caitlin added.

John's mouth hung open, but words failed him completely.

"Are you girls…really interested?" Dani's dad finally asked.

"Absolutely!" the girls answered, with just a tad too much enthusiasm.

Dani could see her dad's eyebrows in the mirror scrunched up with confusion and doubt.

"What kind of mystery could stay a mystery for about a million years, Dad?"

"And who murdered Tom Thomson, sir?" Caitlin asked while attempting to unsmudge the window glass with her T-shirt.

Dani rolled her eyes. "If they knew who murdered Tom Thomson, it wouldn't still be a mystery."

Caitlin folded her arms decisively, felt some dampness on her sleeve, and quickly unfolded them again. "I knew that. Really."

"Well," Dani's dad began, still unsure of his audience, "the first mystery is whether or not he was murdered or simply had an accident. That's been a great Canadian question mark for about eighty-five years, which isn't quite a million years. People were divided over the question of accident versus murder at the time and remain divided today." Another quick glance in the mirror confirmed the interest was genuine.

"How come they still don't know, Dad? I thought murder mysteries were always solved after half a million years or so."

"Well, the thing is, Tom Thomson died under very suspicious circumstances, and there were no witnesses." Dani pulled her trusty journal and pencil out of her knapsack. "Tom drowned in Canoe Lake. But the whole thing's bizarre, really. He was an experienced canoeist and a very good swimmer. The day he died was calm and he was paddling on very familiar waters. But what's strange is that earlier he'd had a dispute with a German fellow named Martin Blecher. They had argued about the war Canada was fighting with Germany. Tom, of course, was a patriot. I think he was a little sensitive to this Blecher fellow's pro-Germany opinions. Tom had been disqualified from active duty because of fallen arches, if you can believe it." John's head did an instantaneous one-eighty, then snapped forward again when they came to some tricky curves in the road.

"Keep going, Dad."

"Wasn't there also some suspicion the butler did it, or in this case the innkeeper?" Bob asked.

"Right you are—Shannon Fraser, the owner of Mowat Lodge. Sixty years after Tom's death, one of the last survivors of that time swore her friend Annie Fraser, who was Shannon's wife, confessed to her that her husband had murdered Tom in an argument over money."

Dani's eyes grew big. "Wow!"

"And after his body was discovered there were a number of very suspicious facts and events that came to light that are still puzzling."

"Like what?" Caitlin asked.

John checked yet again in the mirror to make sure his newly interested listeners weren't pulling his leg. "He had a wound on his right temple as though he'd been struck by a paddle or some other blunt object. His favourite ash paddle was never found, and there was fishing line wrapped around his left ankle sixteen times for no apparent reason. Strangest of all, Tom's constant companion, a sixteen-foot grey-green chestnut canoe, vanished into thin air sometime after they found his body."

"Dad, how in the world do you know all this stuff?"

John chuckled. "Oh, guys just know certain things."

"Didn't you just read about it yesterday in that book Dani got you for your birthday?" Bob asked.

The talking dad looked at the asking dad with sad eyes, sort of the way Nikki did when he accomplished something particularly clever and nobody noticed.

"Oh, yeah," Dani said thoughtfully. "But I thought that book was about mysterious rock formations and junk like that. I didn't know it had interesting stuff like unsolved murders."

"Murder's not supposed to make you so happy, Dani," Caitlin said.

"I'm not happy," Dani said, trying to hide her excitement. "I'm just kind of interested, that's all."

Caitlin giggled. "Oh, sure, Detective Dani."

John tried to recapture the sweet sensation of finally having a fully attentive audience. "Of course, the Ottawa Valley was best known in its early pioneering life for its lumber industry, something few people think about these days. And in truth there really is very little to mark its passing as you drive or boat along the river valley…"

Dani's dad made yet another quick inspection of the back seat to see how he was doing. Nikki continued blissfully unaware in La La Land; Caitlin allowed her eyes to droop as her face gripped the window glass and she drifted once again toward the bottom of the well on a big puffy pillow; Dani wrote ferociously in her journal and smacked her gum, preparing for yet another attempt at the record.

With a grin, and in his deepest radio voice, Bob said, "I'm listening."

John groaned and focused his attention completely on the road for the first time that day. The van climbed and passed St. Mary's Church. The Ottawa River, favoured among rafters because of its thundering whitewater, was flanked by luscious farm fields and the odd gnarly oak tree. The scene, under the noon sun and cumulous clouds, looked as it might have a hundred years ago—not that the girls took any notice. Descending toward Barry's Bay, they motored under ancient pine tress. Colossal columns of sunshine and shadow filtered through the van. Dani's dad whistled through slightly bared teeth, then said, mostly to himself, "What really holds their attention is a complete and utter mystery to me."

2

Are We Having Fun Yet?

After several false starts, the dads managed to build a campfire that didn't immediately go out. The two skinny men slapped each other on the back, coughing and rejoicing at having created a steady source of smoke.

"How come they didn't put the bark and kindling under the logs an hour ago?" Dani asked.

Caitlin shrugged. "Let's face it, dads are weird."

"Yeah, I know, but my dad always tells me how important it is do something right the first time."

"And *my* dad always tells *me* how important it is to do research for school projects," Caitlin added.

Nikki's delicate howl cut into the conversation and through the forest.

"I wonder if our dads researched bringing a dog to Algonquin Park when we talked about leaving Nikki in the kennel," Dani said, pointing to a sign on a wooden post Nikki was leaning against to support his afternoon siesta.

The girls looked up at a large *X* through a happily bounding beagle.

"Oh-oh!" Caitlin said as Nikki planted his chin in the dirt and snorted satisfaction at his lot in life.

"Dad!" Dani cried.

Dani's dad pivoted, a perplexed look on his face, something he always had whenever his daughter used that tone of voice.

The two men walked away from their smoky source of pride and stood for the longest time, slowly moving their heads from Nikki to the sign and back.

"Oh," John simply said.

"Well, what should we do?" Bob countered.

"Um, well, the right thing to do is…that is…" Dani's dad scratched the side of his face while balancing first on one leg, then the other. "Of course, in fairness to park rules, and then again, there *is* Nikki to consider…"

"How about if Caitlin and I take care of hiding Nikki?" Dani offered.

John scrunched his face, mulling over various options, then exhaled. "Okay."

After that the dads stepped back to the source of smoke and said something about perfecting the fire before going on their run.

"Why do you think our dads take running so seriously, Dani?" Caitlin asked.

"'Cause if they don't run, they feel guilty for a week."

Caitlin made her face and neck tense. "'If we don't run today, civilization will cease to exist!'"

Dani giggled. "'But, of course, girls, if you'd like to do something special, well, then, darn it, I can miss a run.

Really, I don't mind!'" But Dani's laugh soon disappeared. "I guess Dad forgot about taking us swimming. He's a great dad..." Dani rubbed her chin. "But sometimes he kind of has the same thing he says Nikki has. You know—ADD, attention-deficit-dog order." She pouted as Nikki howled a truly piercing beagle serenade, which echoed through the pines and across the lake.

Caitlin sniggered. "Well, it's nice to know Nikki's opera lessons are paying off." Then she sighed. "My dad's the same. The world would come to an end if he didn't run, but if the world was really coming to an end, he'd probably just go for a run. Oh, well, maybe they'll relax this week and smell the pinecones, or something like that."

"You know," Dani's dad said as he came up to the girls with Bob in tow, "you should pay attention to some of the things we're doing in case you ever have to fend for yourselves."

"Like, a couple of decades from now," Bob added wistfully.

"God forbid they really have to fend for themselves," John said with resignation.

Dani twisted her face into its most serious expression. "Of course we could fend for ourselves."

"What does *fend* mean?" Caitlin whispered.

"It means you have to be good at outdoor fending," Dani said out of the side of her mouth.

"Oh, right."

"This isn't the city," Dani's dad huffed as Nikki sniffed and snorted. "Out here you have to do things for yourself, act decisively, be in harmony with your environment."

"Well...well...we know how to fend just fine, right, Caitlin?" Dani huffed right back.

"Uh-huh."

"In fact, me and Caitlin were planning to camp out all night by ourselves, right, Caitlin?"

Her friend managed to send her thoughts far, far away as the two dads stood grinning in front of their daughters.

Dani frowned. "Earth to Caitlin, remember our plan to camp out *all* night *all* by ourselves?"

"Oh, sure," Caitlin answered, as if the possibility were as remote as spending a night on the moon.

Dani fumed as her face scrunched into her Pekinese expression. "Caitlin and me are as capable as adults!"

John deepened his voice as he stroked his chin. "Now, Dani, you don't have to get upset. You know you shouldn't be camping out alone before you're ready."

"Watch yourself, John," Bob warned.

With arms folded so tightly they threatened to meet around her back, Dani searched for words and ideas. From her pocket she removed the crumpled map of Canoe Lake they had picked up at the Portage Store. Her eyes widened. "We...we've been planning to camp out at Tom Thomson's favourite campsite—right here."

Caitlin glanced at the map and didn't see any washroom markings.

Thumbing her overalls straps and standing on her toes, Dani said, "So can me and Caitlin—"

"That should be 'May Caitlin and I,'" her father replied, finally unable to resist correcting his daughter's grammar.

Dani came down off her toes and enunciated slowly. "*May* Caitlin and *I* camp out at Tom Thomson's campsite?"

"We're all camping out, Dani."

"We could all check it out this week," Bob suggested.

Dani tried to keep her voice steady. "I *mean*, camping

all by ourselves."

John frowned. "Girls, do you really think that's a good idea at your age?"

Dani levelled her most serious expression in her dad's direction.

"Okay, I get it. Well, I suppose gaining camping experience *is* the reason we're here. Hmm..."

"Come on, John," Bob urged, "what do you say? They both seem so determined!"

Dani placed a victorious hand on Caitlin's terrified shoulder.

Caitlin's look of terror melted into a frown, and she simply said, "Great." Then, as Dani crossed her arms and beamed, a thought occurred to Caitlin. "Just *when* do we have to camp out all by ourselves?"

With her fists clenched deep in her overalls pockets, her shoulders hunched, and her face contorted with determination, Dani said, "Tonight." She liked the sound of *tonight* and continued convincing her audience and herself. "Yeah, we're going to have fun and camp out tonight. Come on, Caitlin, let's go have a man-to-man talk about our plans."

Caitlin skipped along, always a stride behind her friend when there was serious business to attend to. "Dani, are you sure this is a good idea?"

Dani slowed down, her face less Pekinese than pensive. "No, not really."

"Then why did you volunteer us on our first night camping outside ever?"

"Well, what would you like better, facing up to a challenge or having our dads think we don't know how to fend for ourselves?"

Caitlin tugged on her braid while humming softly. "I guess I've never worried too much if Dad thinks I can fend well."

Dani frowned and gave her friend the silent treatment.

Exhaling a big gust of wind, Caitlin said, "Okay, a challenge it is then…I guess. Hey, I just thought of something!" Dani turned slowly and stopped, buoyed by her friend's enthusiasm. "Maybe our dads will think about it and say no and we can pretend we really wanted to camp and fend and stuff like that."

Caitlin grinned triumphantly while Dani jammed her fists into her overalls pockets and strode headlong into the challenge of a lifetime.

3

But Not My Daughter

Each stroke of the paddle sliced into water still and resplendent with summer calm. Snakelike ripples seemed to coil with anger as if to pull the intruder into the depths. Two solitary canoes tentatively glided across black open water. After several minutes' hesitation, the green canoe followed the red into a channel at the north end of the lake. The canoes' tentative approach to their destination belied the determination of their fearless leader.

"This way," Dani called over her shoulder from the stern of the lead canoe.

Perched between father and daughter, Nikki surveyed the lake, looking every bit the captain of the vessel.

"I really don't know about this," Dani's dad said.

Dani sighed. "Dad, you're not really helping."

"Well, I'm sorry, Dani. It's just that I'm a bit worried."

"Dad, you've been encouraging us for a long time to learn outdoor skills—you know, independent stuff," Dani said, never turning her eyes from the distant shore, never wavering in her determination.

Caitlin, in the bow of the green canoe, never wavered in her thoughts about cherry-chocolate gelato.

"It's true, John, their enthusiasm for the outdoor experience is kind of our fault," Bob said.

"Yes, I'm quite happy you girls have decided to take a lesson from the great outdoors and become skilled outdoorswomen, independent and self-reliant. It's just that…" John's voice trailed off as he recited the same objection for the umpteenth time.

"There!" Dani's shout echoed as the canoe rocked and water from her raised paddle soaked Caitlin's head.

"Where?" John said anxiously.

Dani studied her map again. "Yup, I'm sure this is it."

"Where?" John repeated.

Dani let the canoe drift to shore as a look of deep satisfaction spread across her face. "Tom Thomson's favourite campground," she said proudly.

"Oh," John said, torn between continued objection and a sense of shared accomplishment.

The second canoe gently came to rest beside the first on sand and small stones. No one spoke or moved from the canoes. The wayward travellers took in the towering white pines, the sound of cascading water from a nearby stream, and the smell of ripe pine needles.

"No wonder this was Tom's favourite camping spot," Dani said, stepping from the canoe.

"Oh, it's *Tom* now, is it?" John said with a raised eyebrow.

Bob grinned. "So just where is Uncle Tom's cabin, anyway?"

"Look!" Dani cried. "There's a fire pit already built. Come on, Caitlin, let's grab our stuff."

"Fire!" John leaped out of the canoe as if a fire had suddenly been put under his seat.

"Of course, we'll need a fire to cook and to tell stories and to read…" Dani said in a rush.

"And to keep bears away," Caitlin finished with a tad less enthusiasm as she brought up the rear.

John's eyes widened and his Adam's apple bobbed like a fishing lure nibbled by rock bass.

Bob smiled. "It's a pretty safe-looking fire pit, built from stones, no roots showing."

Nikki liked the fire pit, too. He sniffed furiously around it, his snout moving like a vacuum on a cleaning mission.

"We can pitch our tent here," Dani said decisively. "The pine needles will make the ground soft for sleeping. These branches hanging overhead will give us cover in case it rains, and even if the seams of our tent leak, we'll be okay. And we're about the right distance from the fire, close enough to enjoy it, but far enough for safety. What do you think, Caitlin?"

Caitlin unceremoniously spat out one of her wet French braids and slurped, "Charming, I'm sure."

Dani's face reconfigured into a deep frown.

John saw his opening, put one arm around each girl, and said in a fatherly tone. "You know, girls, you really don't have to do this. Twelve-year-old girls, after all…"

Bob winced and patted his friend on the back. "Good luck, buddy."

Dani folded her arms in silent protest, while Caitlin looked around nervously for a washroom.

John peered at his daughter. "What?"

"*Girls!*" Dani stated emphatically.

"Washroom?" Caitlin asked in a softer voice to no one in particular. She vaguely wondered, *If you said* washroom *in the forest and nobody heard it, did you really say it?* But simmering campground discussion meant there was no more time for pondering philosophical questions.

"No, no, it's your age I'm concerned with, not the fact you're *girls*...really," John pleaded to an unsympathetic jury.

Air snorted out of Dani's nose in not-so-silent protest.

John looked at his determined daughter and her distracted friend and decided he was outnumbered. All at once he let out a great breath of air, his shoulders sagged, and his eyes watered ever so slightly. "Okay, girls, you win. You can camp out tonight." And then, with his Adam's apple bobbing, he added, "That is, all night, and you'll be fine, I'm sure."

Dani's flaring nostrils relaxed, while Caitlin's searching eyes fixed on a pile of pine needles she reluctantly conceded were to become their "natural" washroom.

"Well, John," Bob began, "maybe we should leave these capable outdoorspersons to prepare their campsite and settle in for the night."

Panic fluttered across John's face, but then he calmed himself with a couple of deep breaths and simply said, "Okay."

As the men paddled into the Algonquin sunset, the girls could clearly hear one dad reassuring the other. With each assurance John asked, "But do you think they'll really be okay, Bob?"

"Dad sure can be a pain sometimes," Dani said.

"Sure hope my dad's right," Caitlin thought out loud.

"Of course he's right," Dani asserted, half believing her own words.

"Yeah, I guess," Caitlin concluded, not believing a word. "What could possibly happen?"

A large raven pierced the summer silence with a shriek as it lifted from the limb of a pine. The girls jumped and laughed nervously as wings flapped overhead.

Dani giggled. "That's right, Caitlin. What could possibly happen?"

"Oh, only everything," Caitlin whispered, looking up into the shaking pine branches.

4
The Hour of the Dead

Caitlin's trepidation increased as the distant canoe with the only adults in about a million miles faded from sight. And because they couldn't go back until morning Caitlin felt real panic. Naturally she communicated this fear directly to her best friend.

"Guess we can't get gelato here, huh?"

Dani understood her friend's fear and harboured some anxiety herself. Naturally she communicated this back. "No, but I'll bet we could paddle across Canoe Lake, then hitchhike to Ottawa and be back before it gets really dark."

The girls looked at each other and smiled weakly.

"Come on, Caitlin, let's set up our tent. It'll be fine, really," Dani said, meaning there was no way they could get back now, and besides, how could they face their dads if they went back early?

"Well, I guess the campsite is okay and the sunset is getting real pretty," Caitlin said, meaning they weren't nearly as pretty as an outhouse would be right about now.

The girls worked hard for the next thirty minutes, setting up their tent, gathering fallen branches, hauling a bucket of water, and setting it beside the fire pit. Nikki followed first Dani and then Caitlin around the campsite, sniffing and watching with keen interest as the girls fended for themselves. Caitlin struggled to figure our where the heck all the contraptions that came with the tent were supposed to go. Dani smiled to herself, thinking about her dad asking Bob for about the millionth time, "But will they remember to bring water up from the lake to keep from burning down the forest?" The moment the tent was finally erected Nikki plunged in for his beauty sleep.

As they sat beside a steady fire in the great outdoors, the girls thought their gourmet meal of hot dogs and marshmallows tasted especially good. Their dads had packed a large salad, but the girls had forgotten about it until they had eaten their marshmallows.

"Maybe we'll want some for breakfast," Dani suggested.

"And maybe there's a washroom with a Jacuzzi just beyond those trees," Caitlin said, drawing circles in the air with the smoke from her marshmallow stick.

After the ripening sunset stripped the last shades of purple and orange from the sky, the girls settled into their sleeping bags for the night. Talk within the tent was punctuated by an assortment of strange sounds outside.

Whenever Caitlin asked, "What's that?" as she tended to do every few minutes, Dani answered with calming words in an anxious voice: "They're just the *natural* sounds of the forest."

Dani had heard this line in a documentary film once.

She vaguely wondered if the film had meant *spooky* instead of *natural*. For a while the girls were quiet, listening to the forest and the sounds of their own breathing. They could hear frogs croaking, the gentle lapping of water on the shore, and the buzzing of mosquitoes close to their ears.

"Caitlin, they're just a few sounds we're going to have to get used to. In fact, we're already getting—" A piercing hoot cut through the forest. Each girl grabbed the other, naturally, to shield herself from the eerie, *natural* sound. "It's…it's…it's okay," Dani stammered. "Just…just an owl."

Caitlin released her grip on her friend. "How the heck do skunks and porcupines ever sleep around here at night?"

Dani rolled her eyes and wondered, *If you roll your eyes in the dark and no one sees you do it, did it really happen?* "Caitlin, skunks and porcupines don't sleep at night. They sleep during the day."

"Naturally," Caitlin said.

"It's 'cause they're *nocturnal*," Dani said in the matter-of-fact voice she always used when she was trying to impress.

"No, Dani, it's 'cause of all the racket," Caitlin countered. "It makes them all natural insomniacs, and us, too."

"Caitlin, I'm sure we'll soon be used to the sounds—" Dani's voice went shrill as the great horned owl continued its serenade.

Caitlin laughed hysterically, and soon Dani managed a giggle. "Okay, so it may take a few months to get used to the sounds, We'll just have to stay here until we do."

The girls lay awake talking and listening for a long time. Eventually exhaustion displaced fear and they drifted into deep, satisfying sleep. For about five minutes.

"You awake, Dani?"

"Yeah, how 'bout you?"

"No, I'm asleep. I'm talking in my sleep 'cause you hypnotized me, or else the owl did. Maybe you can check for me."

Dani ignored her friend's early-morning sarcasm. "I'm not even tired."

"Neither am I," Caitlin said with excitement, "and it's still nighttime."

Dani lifted the tent flap. Whispers of light had begun to filter through the darkness. "We're in the Hour of the Dead," she said in her most serious voice.

"Huh?" Caitlin said, truly puzzled.

Dani continued in a serious and dramatic voice. "It's the beginning of dawn, and I read that this is the time when most people die."

"Wow," Caitlin whispered.

"It's the time when the world is most calm, so people leave this mortal coil." Dani remembered hearing a guy called Hamlet talk like that.

"Or else people die 'cause it's so spooky outside," Caitlin added, but Dani was alone with her thoughts. "Hey, Dani, I'm not even tired. Maybe it should be called the Hour of the Wide Awake."

Dani snapped back to the world of the living. "You know, you're right. I'm wide awake, too. Come on, let's go outside and look around."

"Ah…" But before Caitlin could finish her objection Dani was out of the tent. When Nikki also roused himself with a world-record yawn and stretch, Caitlin concluded she had no choice but to check out this hour-of-the-dead thing. The girls stood listening to, without seeing, hundreds of birds screeching and flapping about overhead as if the entire world were already awake and eager to greet the new day. A shroud of mist lay across the entire lake and campsite.

"Wow!" Dani said.

"You can say that again," Caitlin agreed.

"Wow!" Dani obliged. "It's so…"

"Spooky."

"Beautiful," Dani whispered.

"Spooky," Caitlin whispered.

Close to the girls but lost to the mist came a slap and a flapping of wings. The pair were startled and then mesmerized by the long, eerie sound of a loon puncturing the dull blanket of mist.

"Spooky," Dani said.

"It's so beautiful," Caitlin said, her thoughts finally no longer preoccupied with outhouses.

The cry of the loon echoed across the lake unmuffled by the mistlike waves lapping the shore. As the echo faded, it seemed as if everything had stopped. The girls let out a breath together. As a second cry erupted, they strained to see through the mist and emerging light.

"There," Dani said, pointing toward a noise coming from somewhere within the thick mist. But this sound wasn't from a loon. The girls heard a whiz followed by a dull plop. As the pair searched the mist for the source, a shape slowly emerged.

"Something floating," Dani said, straining on her tiptoes.

"Could be an outhouse," Caitlin offered, reverting to her old obsession.

Dani was about to speak when the shape disappeared altogether.

Again they heard a distinct whiz followed by a dull plop. The girls leaned forward, each holding an overhanging branch to keep from falling into the water.

"I've been counting. It's been about seventy seconds between whizzes," Dani observed.

"Interesting," Caitlin said. *Every little mystery's got to be figured out by that girl*, she thought.

Dani leaned farther into the mist, determined to discover the source of the mysterious sounds and shape. Caitlin was about to comment on the precarious angle of Dani's leaning but was struck by an amusing thought: *The Leaning Tower of Dani*. Caitlin was about to share her amusing thought when her friend's branch snapped and Dani did a belly flop into the lake. Although only knee-deep, Dani shouted from the shock of her cold morning swim. She splashed wildly, and Caitlin almost followed her friend as she put a hand over her mouth, forgetting she, too, was suspended over the water from a tree twig. Just as Dani quit flailing in the water and attempted to pull herself out, both girls heard a distinct voice exclaim, "Darn!"

Dani stood completely still, dripping, shivering, and listening.

"Did you hear that, Dani?" Caitlin whispered loudly.

As Dani opened her mouth to speak, a shape emerged from the mist. A battered grey-green canoe came straight toward where Dani stood, without causing the slightest ripple in the water. Even before the back of the canoe appeared, the girls detected the sweet smell of tobacco.

Dani was about to reach out and touch the bow of the canoe when she glimpsed the figure of a man seated at the stern. Just as the boat was about to drift into Dani, the dark figure gave a barely perceptible turn of the paddle and it veered away. As the girls attempted to collect their scattered wits and fend for themselves by screaming and running, the dark stranger uttered a single word: "Mornin'."

The stranger placed the paddle he gripped in his right hand and the fishing rod he held in his left hand on the thwart of the canoe. Then he placed his elbows in his lap and calmly removed the pipe between his teeth. While the girls stared, he searched in his shirt for a box of matches and carefully relit his pipe. The girls waited anxiously for the stranger to speak. Instead he puffed on his pipe until he seemed satisfied it was well lit. With a blank expression on his face, he muttered, this time through clenched teeth, "Mornin'."

Dani desperately wanted to tell this intrusive stranger how frightening he and his phantom canoe were to two twelve-years-olds out for a walk or swim during the Hour of the Dead on their first-ever camping trip all by themselves. Caitlin wanted to scream because it seemed the right thing to do somehow. But both girls were disarmed by the simple greeting from a stranger who hardly seemed to notice them at all. They wanted to take decisive action, but found themselves just saying "Morning." The girls were even more confused as the stranger touched two fingers to the peak of his worn hat and slightly bowed his head.

Dani decided she'd had enough. "What the...who do you...why in the world?"

Caitlin decided to complement her friend's effort. "We wondered...I mean, we thought...and it sure is early, don't you think?"

The stranger's pipe moved along clenched teeth from one side to the other. "You're scarin' the fish away." No reproach or threat, just a statement of fact.

"We scared…we scared…we scared…" As Dani finished saying *scared* for the third time, the branch Caitlin was holding snapped and she fell, rather dramatically, into the water. After Caitlin's splashing and screaming subsided, the stranger muttered, "Yup, that'll scare 'em, all right."

Caitlin finally steadied herself, placed her dripping hands on her dripping hips, and said, "If we scared the fish, mister, it's 'cause you scared the living daylights—or nightlights—out of us, whoever you are." Caitlin finished her sentence with a dripping snort.

For the first time the stranger seemed to look at the soaking, dishevelled mess the girls had become. The trace of a smile creased his lips through bared teeth as he slowly removed his pipe and said, "Name's Tom. Tom Thomson."

5
Something's Fishy

Nikki expressed his feelings about not being part of all the commotion by bellowing into an otherwise calm Hour of the Dead. The stranger's eyes lifted slowly to the shore. "Dog's good for huntin'."

Dani attempted to summon the courage to speak to the stranger claiming to be Tom Thomson. A number of reasonable arguments aimed at persuading the scary man in the canoe to leave worked their way through her methodical mind. She hooked a hand through each of her soaking overall straps in final preparation for speech. But as she opened her mouth, Caitlin answered the stranger.

"His name's Nikki, and he's never hunted before. He doesn't know how, and we wouldn't want him to learn, right, Dani? Say, what's your *real* name, mister?" Then, looking back at her exasperated friend, Caitlin said, "Gosh, Dani, did you know your teeth are chattering?"

Dani's teeth continued to chatter as her eyes rolled. She

opened her mouth to speak a second time, but the stranger spoke instead.

"Catch a cold if you stay in the water, girls."

Dani swiped at a wet strand of hair on her forehead and folded her arms. "And we could die of fright from strange men appearing at our campsite in the middle of the night."

Dani's protestation finished on a shrill, angry note. The stranger's eyebrows moved together into a slight frown as his pipe played upon his ivory keyboard.

"I thought you said it was the Hour of the Dead, Dani," Caitlin observed. "And look, there's a bit of pink and yellow over where the sun's gonna come up."

Dani plunged her hands into overalls pockets that now had the consistency of used diapers. An inaudible "yuck" crossed her lips as she promptly removed both hands and held them unnaturally by her sides. A little giggle escaped Caitlin's lips but not Dani's attention. "Caitlin! This isn't a laughing matter."

"I know," Caitlin said, giggling, "but it is kind of silly."

Dani bared her teeth as if she held a pipe in her own mouth, then motioned her eyes toward the stranger. "Caitlin," she whispered, "we have to keep our wits about us."

"And apparently to ourselves," Caitlin replied.

"Sorry, girls. Didn't mean to scare ya. Didn't hardly know how to approach. Thought this might be a good time."

"'Cause it's the Hour of the Dead," Caitlin said, wide-eyed.

"Nope. 'Cause it's the best time for fishin'."

"Oh," Caitlin said with obvious disappointment.

"Been fishin' round here a long, long time." The stranger's eyes moved slightly in both directions as if to survey the lake. "Used to camp at this…at your campsite pretty often. Was my favourite."

"But you don't camp here anymore? Is there something wrong with this campsite, mister? Do you know of a better one?" Caitlin asked as she might question the librarian about the latest exciting kid's novel.

"This here campsite's the best," the stranger said, motioning with his pipe in his mouth. "Don't camp anymore. Can't. Just travel in this old canoe."

"You mean all day, everyday, you just paddle, fish, and smoke your pipe?"

The stranger nodded. "And all night." Then, with a slight, ironic smile curled on his lips, he added, "Even during the Hour of the Dead."

Caitlin shivered and shuddered. "But for heaven's sake, why?"

During this exchange, and no doubt partly because of the soggy conditions, Dani fidgeted, fussed, and fumed. Now she asserted herself with big words and big splashes as she clambered up the clammy shore. "I'm sorry, mister, but the thing, is we're terribly busy at our campsite, since we're part of an outdoor-education program and we're improving our self-improvement—"

"We are?" Caitlin's question was greeted by an exasperated look from her friend. "Dani, are you okay? 'Cause you kinda sound like your dad."

Dani enunciated her words in her best elder-sister, know-it-all voice. *"Yes, we are Caitlin."* And then she said to the stranger, "We're involved in an outdoor-education program with our school, and we expect our teachers, all twenty of them, here any minute, 'cause they're going to evaluate our camping performance. So maybe you better just keep on fishing."

Caitlin's feigned whisper echoed across the lake. "Wow, Dani, you sound just like our older, bossy sisters, but you're talking like this stranger, with your teeth kind of clenched."

Dani opened her mouth to speak, but dramatically folded her arms instead when Caitlin continued with another quick question to the stranger.

"Say, mister, what was the reason you said for canoeing, fishing, and smoking your whole life?" Caitlin cocked her head to one side with real beaglelike puzzlement.

The stranger surveyed the girls, the campsite, and the emerging glimmer of light for several moments in silence. The pipe slowly worked its way along his white teeth once again before being removed with great care. His expressive eyes belied his placid expression as he searched for words. "Never did say what the reason was. Hardly know how to start. Best to come to the point." And then he curled his lip slightly and revealed a hint of a smile. "Never been good at painting pictures with words."

"Huh?" both girls said.

The crease of a smile disappeared, and the stranger drew a deep breath from the vaporous mist. "My name is Tom Thomson. I have canoed, fished, and smoked my pipe on this lake since I was murdered on July 8, 1917. And if you help me prove my murder to the world once and for all, I'll make you a warm fire and cook breakfast with these fine fellows."

The stranger, or Tom Thomson, held up a chain with two big fish hanging from it. With their dead eyes and large mouths grotesquely open, the fish resembled, only a little, the girls who stood agape and wide-eyed in front of them.

6
Breakfast of Champions

A warm, inviting fire crackled as brilliant early sunlight burned mist from the still lake. The girls, dressed in dry clothes, ate fresh lake trout with voracious appetites. The stranger—or Tom Thomson, which was even stranger—watched the girls devour the fish he had caught and cooked, his pipe playing along his teeth and a warm smile dancing at the corners of his eyes and mouth. Even though the circumstances of their togetherness felt odd, a comfortable mood had settled among the threesome as they nestled beside the fire in full view of the lake and the splendour of the awakening day.

As she finished smacking an enormous mouthful of fish, Dani noted that the expression on the stranger's face had changed from solemn to smiling. She thought the situation was perhaps too calm for comfort. "Mister, that was the best fish I ever ate!"

Caitlin smiled with satisfaction and smacked her own

lips. The stranger made a slight courteous bow.

Tom's old grey hat sat at the back of his head, hardly noticed since he had pinned on one of his homemade fishing lures more than eighty years ago. Tom's decrepit pants were the colour of charred wood, far removed from their original beige. His elbow showed through his flannel shirt, a dulled plaid of washed-out red and indistinguishable white.

They look like they're a hundred years old, Caitlin thought, which was pretty close to the truth.

Hope I can make my overalls last that long, Dani mused hopefully.

With her plate now clean, Dani was ready to become serious again. She grabbed the straps of her clean, dry overalls to show earnest intent and to wipe her sticky fingers. Her chest heaved as she formulated the question for her interrogation but, caught between comfort and confusion, she hesitated. Finally she simply asked, "What the heck are you smiling at, mister?"

The stranger's playful smile remained as he knocked his pipe against a campfire rock. All three watched as a clump of stale tobacco and ashes tumbled into the flame. The stranger refilled his pipe slowly, deliberately, and after a time responded to Dani, who waited, and Caitlin, who chewed. "I think...I understand your dilemma."

Dani rocked and held her straps. "And which dilemma would that be?"

"The one your mind is now fishin' round to solve."

Dani huffed and puffed as she paced around the fire. She then let out a breath of air and sunk to the ground, her cheeks in the palms of her hands, which finally came to rest on her knees.

The stranger pushed his hat back farther and took a deep breath. Then he began his narrative, secure in the knowledge that his trout breakfast had earned the girls' attention. "I can imagine that all this—me here now—must be sort of..."

"Weird," Dani offered.

"Silly," Caitlin suggested.

"Confusing," the stranger finished.

The three breakfast companions looked at one another and smiled.

The mysterious fisherman continued. "This all must seem confusing, weird, and silly. And I know it may be difficult to believe I'm Tom Thomson but—" he became solemn and placed his pipe between his teeth "—I know you both would like to say I can't be who I say I am, yet I bet you still remember your experience earlier this summer with Walter MacNeill."

The contents of Dani's latest mouthful of trout were expelled with jet propulsion. Caitlin fell backward from the log she had been contentedly sitting on. Nikki looked up from his fish remains, howled once at the uproar, and quickly returned his limited attention to the object of his unlimited desire.

"But how...what...who...when...why?" the astonished girls asked together through semi-filled mouths. After which a long silence enveloped the tranquil campsite.

"Your good deeds in finally freeing Walter MacNeill from his murder at Summerhouse are known to those of us who are still lookin' for a way—a place—to lay down the paddle and rest."

The girls gasped. "You mean you're dead just like Mr. MacNeill?" Caitlin tentatively asked.

"Yup."

"And," Caitlin continued with heightened curiosity, "in the dead zone do you guys talk about, you know, stuff like how we helped Mr. MacNeill?"

The stranger was thoughtful as he replaced his pipe. "No, we don't talk exactly, don't know anything about each other unless..." He paused seemingly forever, then said, "Part of the problem of remaining a spirit is that we're caught in a small part of our own lives that we must continue to live until we resolve it. Fact is, I'm bored with my life that was and want to move on."

Caitlin was confused. "But then how did you find out about us and Mr. MacNeill? It doesn't make sense." Caitlin crossed her arms to complete the picture of profound puzzlement.

The stranger slowly responded with a smile. "It's true. It doesn't make sense—if sense is what yer lookin' for. Did your adventure with Walter MacNeill make sense?" Caitlin's arms dropped as the stranger continued. "And it won't make sense any more than, than—" the stranger turned toward the lake "—painting what you see here would make sense to someone who can only see a photograph. You have to feel something first, the essence of the thing, and then you have to believe in it, have faith in the thing and in yourself. Especially in yourself, 'cause no one else is going to see it unless you do first, and even then they might not."

"Huh?" Caitlin asked in bewilderment.

Dani had been stroking her chin, considering carefully

what the stranger was saying. "Well, I guess if Mr. MacNeill's story is known somewhere, somehow, and Caitlin and I know it happened, even though we can't tell anyone we know, at least any adult we know, well, then, I guess that's good enough for me. What do you say, Caitlin?"

"Huh?" Caitlin repeated. Then a knowing expression crossed her face. "Oh, I get it. You want to be a detective again, don't you?"

Dani's left eyebrow lifted high as the beginning of a smile unfolded. "Well…maybe. Don't you?"

Caitlin instinctively began to chew one of her French braids. "That depends, I guess."

The stranger nodded, removed his pipe, and used it like a pointer or a paintbrush. "I think if I explain a few things it might help. I mean, you can't paint a picture till you see it, right?"

"You mean *feel* it," Caitlin corrected.

The stranger smiled with satisfaction.

Dani half stated and half asked, "You really *are* Tom Thomson, aren't you, mister?"

"Yup."

"My dad says although it's still a mystery, most people believe you probably died from an accident." Dani dropped her voice to a whisper. "He says the truth is, most fishermen die with their flies down, meaning they fall into the water trying to go to the bathroom." Dani continued with enthusiasm. "Mr. Thomson, how are you going to prove you were murdered?"

Tom Thomson sighed with resignation. "I know what people think, what historians have written." Then he said, bristling with anger, "But it's not true. And I can't prove I was murdered. Only you two can." He nodded at each girl. "If you're willin'."

Dani grabbed her overalls straps and grinned while Caitlin chewed her braids and moaned. A steady, powerful flapping of wings diverted the group's attention from the campsite to calm water still shrouded in morning mist. A great blue heron rose from the vapour and flew toward the campsite before veering slowly and deliberately away from the trio.

"So beautiful," Caitlin observed.

"A sign," Dani speculated.

"The heron may well be a sign, and it's good that you 'blessed it unaware,'" the stranger said.

"Huh?" Dani blurted.

"Felt its beauty. I never could paint one of those birds."

Dani stood, overalls straps in hand. "Never mind that...Mr. Thomson. We have work to do. Now tell us what needs to get done."

"And how?" Caitlin meekly added.

Tom smiled fully for the first time since appearing through the mist. "I thought you'd never ask."

7
The Painted Word

"For many reasons, the time to prove, to correct, history is finally here," Tom said.

Nikki glanced up at the girls conversing with nothing but morning air, thought all was well, snorted, and proceeded to create another bed at Dani's feet. As the dog's head came to rest on Dani's running shoe and his eyes glazed over, Tom continued. "It's not just that you two are here at Canoe Lake now." He leaned forward, and an intensity not shown before entered his voice. "You see, a historian is here now, as well, tryin' to get a sense of the place before writin' a book—a very influential book that will lure public opinion away from the truth." He bit down on the pipe in his mouth and stewed for a moment.

Removing his pipe, Tom spat out, "Just 'cause he has a Ph.D. and has written a few books, he's takin' the high and mighty opinion that I died from an accident, plain and simple." He shoved the pipe back into his mouth, nearly chipping a tooth. "Professor Fairburn and his assistant are tryin'—"

"Wow!" Dani practically shouted. "Did you say Professor Fairburn, as in Professor Dustin Fairburn?"

"Yup."

"But...but...we, me and Caitlin—that is, Caitlin and I—know Dustin Fairburn."

Tom nodded. "I know. I did mention something about timing bein' right."

"But Dustin Fairburn has a Ph.D. And he's a professor, a famous historian, and we're just two, two..."

"Seasoned detectives," Tom finished.

A light bulb went off in Dani's head and she glowed. "Oh, yeah."

Caitlin remained unconvinced. "But...?"

Tom held up his pipe as if to paint away any objection. "Let me explain first, please."

The girls tried to hold still while Tom sighed and continued calmly. "There have been many theories, historical accounts over the years. I never in a million years would have thought I could cause such a commotion. But then people just plain gave up tryin' to find a reason for my sudden death..." He let his voice trail off, lost in his private reverie. "People said it was a mystery, too long ago, and there wasn't enough evidence to actually solve what they called a bizarre mystery. I'm so sick of that word *mystery* when common sense and a decent Scout could find..." Tom's eyes narrowed as he became agitated. "Some misguided people even speculated I might have committed suicide because Winnifred Trainor was pregnant! Well, she never was, and what kind of a fool would end his own life as a solution to something he'd done, anyway?" Again Tom reined his temper in, then whispered, "And besides, we were only ever just friends. But people never understood that."

Caitlin held her hands to her mouth, then burst out, "You didn't love her? Did she love you?"

Tom seemed genuinely perturbed by the directness of the questions. "Well I…sort of, but then…" He squinted as though deep in thought. "Winnie and I were very good friends but, no, I didn't love her. You see, I fell in love once when I was in Seattle—flat-out rejected. Hurt more than a kick in the head by a mule and I said never again. Poor Winnie didn't know this about me, came to believe I could settle down. I might not have been that fair to her, but all this is beside the point."

Dani was about to ask a question about this Winnifred Trainor character when Tom continued. "But the answer is right there. Historians are supposed to be able to figure stuff like this out, aren't they?" He glared at the girls, who were unable to agree or disagree.

Finally Dani's detective mind formulated a question to the question. "Figure out exactly what, Mr. Thomson?"

"Why, who the murderer is, of course. And if you don't mind, it's Tom, just Tom."

Caitlin spat out a well-chewed braid, spread her hands dramatically, and asked, "Do you mean historians who have written books and who have Ph.D.s couldn't actually solve this mystery—I mean, find out who murdered you?"

Anger, or at least agitation, registered in Tom's eyes even as a hint of a smile traced his mouth. He nodded at each girl. "But you and you could."

Dani and Caitlin practically shouted, "What!" before levelling more polite but equally felt protestations. "You can't mean us. We couldn't. They don't give out Ph.D.s in grade six."

Tom looked at the girls intensely and said with absolute certainty. "I spent the best years of my life in Algonquin Park lookin' for something in nature I can't even begin to describe...in words. There were moments I can still remember, can still feel, and I came close to puttin' only a small number of those down on canvas before I died. I had this idea early in 1917 that I would sketch or paint something every day all spring and into the summer and fall to show the change of seasons—colours, shapes, shades—little by little. I wanted to reveal something of real mystery, the beauty and wonder of life. A darn Ph.D. isn't the thing. What a person's made up of is what counts. I know what you and you—" he nodded again "—are made up of, and I know you can prove I was murdered, show the world who it was, and set the record straight."

Caitlin and Dani looked at each other: baffled, scared, but reluctant to disappoint Tom's faith in them.

"But..." Caitlin began.

"How?" Dani completed.

Tom relaxed, smiled at the girls, and even took time to relight his pipe as the girls waited, frozen. "Why, the diary, of course."

8
The Hermit of Canoe Lake

The girls' triumphant return to base camp was overshadowed by agitation from their dads.

"Hey, girls!" Dani's dad said, hurrying over. "We were just getting ready to come and get you."

Bob whistled. "Back by 9:00 a.m. I'm impressed. How'd the outdoor experience go?"

"It was a cinch," Dani said from the tips of her toes.

"It was very *spirit*ual," Caitlin said slyly.

Both dads' eyebrows arched. "Huh?"

"Well, never mind that now. Bob and I spotted a dangerous criminal on our morning run and we just reported him to the park warden's office." John stood on one nervous leg and then the other as Bob's Adam's apple bobbed. Together they were a portrait of nervous energy.

"Turns out he's been robbing campgrounds and the Portage Store," Bob said. "Rumour is, he's been hiding in the woods for years. Ha, the Hermit of Canoe Lake. Has a nice ring to it, don't you think?"

John's curled eyebrow conveyed annoyance. "He could be armed and he's definitely dangerous."

"How do you know he's dangerous, Dad?" Dani asked.

"Experience, dear, experience."

Dani attempted to change the subject. "We had fun camping and fending, Dad."

But the two men were fixed on the finer points of criminal searches.

Dani continued under her breath. "We only met the most famous artist in the world, who also happens to be dead just now and who casually mentioned he wouldn't mind us helping solve his murder and then convince the world of the truth. Really quite uneventful, all told."

Caitlin giggled. "Quite."

Suddenly John turned toward the girls, having convinced Bob of his important point, and said in his deepest, gravest voice. "Bob and I want you girls to take every precaution. We don't know what we're dealing with here."

"From now on," Bob said, "we want you to stick together and stay in touch with us with this cellphone. I'm giving you mine, and we'll have John's. Carry it with you at all times."

"We've called the park warden and he should be here in a few minutes." An old Toyota Land Cruiser bumped through a series of potholes and slammed to a stop in a cloud of dust. John's jaw hung motionless.

Someone coughed inside the truck. Dust continued to engulf the Toyota as an official-looking man emerged in a hurry, attempting to pull his leather belt over his sizable belly. His stride slowed and he completed the manoeuvre, cheeks puffed out, satisfied with the effort. However, with his next step the belt and pants slid over his girth again, making him look less official but a whole lot more comfortable. Sunglasses spread across a wide nose, and a sad moustache drooped over a tiny mouth. The label on his shirt read: PARK WARDEN.

"Afternoon. Name's Willins, Warden Willins. Understand youse had some trouble here." Beads of sweat cascaded from his bald head.

There go the pants again, Dani thought. But as she watched the warden take official control of the investigation, she felt something at her feet. Nikki lifted his head from its habitual resting place on her shoe, smacked and licked his lips several times without opening his eyes, then thumped back into Beagleland with a loud canine snort.

Caitlin and Dani drew breaths at the same time as they realized the park warden would most certainly throw the whole group out of the park if he saw Nikki. *An illegal beagle alien*, Caitlin thought.

Nikki shook himself to life as Dani gently pulled his head off her shoe by his collar. The dog rotated three times in an attempt to rediscover blissful sleep on Dani's shoe before being assertively escorted from the investigation with his front paws dangling in the air.

"Caitlin, grab his leash." Dani huffed with exertion as Nikki hopped reluctantly alongside his master.

"That was close," Caitlin whispered, brushing twigs off her clothes and noticing for the first time that camping wasn't particularly complimentary to her appearance.

Dani looked over her shoulder at the three men in deep conversation in the distance. "Wow, that was way too close, but since our dads look like they're going to be busy for a while, maybe now's the perfect time for us to make our move."

"Perfect time for what?" Caitlin asked distractedly, thinking about lunch.

"Operation Running Shoe," Dani said in her most matter-of-fact detective voice.

"Oh," Caitlin said. She thought for a moment. "Why?"

"To take our dads' running shoes and show them there's more to life than running."

"Oh." Caitlin thought for another moment. "But I thought detectives were supposed to find stuff, not lose it."

Dani sighed heavily. "It depends. Detectives work all kinds of ways."

"Oh." Caitlin wondered for yet another moment. "I see." But, of course, she didn't see anything at all.

Dani and Caitlin crept over to the tents where they found four pairs of running shoes.

"Now unless our skinny dads have shoes stashed at the back of the toilet, this should do it," Dani said proudly.

Caitlin pined for a toilet but asked, "Now what do we do?"

"We hide these shoes where even the chipmunks can't find them," Dani said, already heading for the forest faster than her dad on a run.

"Oh, Dani," Caitlin called in a singsong voice, "aren't you forgetting something?"

"Huh?" Dani's confusion was given immediate relief by a tree-shattering beagle howl. "Ten on the Richter scale," she groaned.

"Sad thing is, he's got an eleven in him just dying to come out," Caitlin deadpanned.

After Dani's face registered a multitude of horrors, she grabbed Nikki's leash and prepared for flight. "Come on, Caitlin, before we get into double trouble."

Interesting idea, Caitlin thought. *Double trouble trying to stay out of double trouble*. As she fell in behind Dani's long stride, she muttered, "If a beagle howls in the forest and nobody hears it, did it really happen?"

"What did you say?" Dani asked.

"Don't ask," Caitlin answered.

A couple of hundred feet away a bead of sweat hit a pad of paper. "What in tarnation…? Was that a beagle?"

John looked guilty, veins popping as he shrugged.

"I don't think so," Bob answered, hoping the warden would leave soon so they could chow down after their run.

"Mighta been a coyote, but sure sounded like a—"

"Basset hound," John offered.

"No. A beagle. Sounded more like that. But, heck, nobody'd be dumb enough to bring a dog camping, else they'd be throw'd out."

Another bead hit the warden's pad, blurring the ink. "I'd go have a look, but I best get on this case right away. I won't rest till I've solved it." The good warden let another bead fall, pretty well obscuring everything he'd written. "'Cause if there's one thing I can't stand, it's an unsolved case on my turf."

"We have every faith in you, Warden," John said.

The two dads' mouths and moods dropped ever so slightly as the belt buckle once again descended below the warden's belly with the inevitability of the sun setting on a beautiful August evening in Algonquin Park.

9
A Talk in the Woods

“You can’t see the forest for the running shoes,” Caitlin announced, hands on her hips as she surveyed her handiwork. Eight running shoes hung strategically from two magnificent spruce trees.

Dani admired the arrangement for a moment before pivoting with Nikki in tow, intent upon their next adventure. “Diary,” she said enthusiastically, ignoring Caitlin altogether. “Our work is done here. Now we have to find out about a diary written around the time of Tom Thomson’s death and then analyze it carefully.”

Caitlin groaned to deaf ears and vaguely thought, *If you groan in the forest and nobody hears—nah!*

“Earth to Caitlin!” Dani called to her friend. She was a full stride ahead as the girls hurtled headlong through campsites looking for their first lead in the case. “Let’s review our plan.” She pulled her hands out of her overall pockets and smashed a determined fist into her other hand.

"Dani, calm down!" Caitlin said, abruptly halting and folding her arms with equal determination.

Dani continued walking vigorously, strategically reviewing options and otherwise enjoying being a detective again.

"Dani!" Caitlin called out after her first protest went unnoticed.

"Wha—" Dani stopped midstride and midsentence. "Caitlin, what the heck are you doing back there? We have work to do!"

"Hmm," Caitlin said to no one in particular. She refolded her arms as dramatically as she could without appearing to be hugging herself.

"Well?" Dani waited.

"At least you stopped for one second," Caitlin conceded.

"Caitlin, we're probably getting close to Dustin Fairburn's campsite. The warden said it's—" Dani studied a map produced from the depths of her overalls "—about four hundred yards past the bay we just passed."

"Then I am truly sorry, Miss Kennedy," a familiar, uncontrite voice said through the bushes. "A different academic approach, a new innovative research method—yes, these I could tolerate, for I am not an inflexible academic, but to adopt a viewpoint for your thesis without a shred of evidence beyond these circumstantial musings and, I dare say, in direct opposition to my own research and anticipated book, well, that I simply cannot tolerate."

The girls inhaled deeply.

"Dustin," Dani said on a high note.

"Fairburn," Caitlin finished on a low note for dramatic contrast.

"However, Professor Fairburn," a determined voice

countered, "as you know, there's never been anything except circumstantial evidence for over eighty years, and surely the integrity of academic research and discourse exists in the lively exchange of differing views."

A sharp tone crept into Dustin Fairburn's controlled voice. "Miss Kennedy, I hardly have to remind you that I am familiar with the need for academic freedom and tolerance. Of course, one may adopt an opposing voice to the prevailing notion, even if it is unorthodox. However, academic research implies the presence of research findings, and I must point out, Miss Kennedy, an academic advising relationship requires compatibility in fundamental outlook which, I must say, is altogether lacking between us on this question."

There was a pause, then the shaky but determined voice continued. "Are you saying, Professor Fairburn, that you won't supervise my thesis simply because I disagree with you?"

"Precisely. Oh, I know you think me harsh, Miss Kennedy, but it is simply that I cannot, in good conscience, continue. And let me remind you that this wayward path you are embarking on is a reversal of your earlier intentions."

"Yes," the young voice answered with less determination and more emotion. "I've changed my views based on research...and intuition."

"Dear me," an exasperated Fairburn said. "The research I shall offer in my book is sound and will support the accepted view. I am truly sorry, Miss Kennedy, but I must really get back to work. I am certain one of the new faculty members can take you on. Now, if you will excuse me, please."

"Certainly," she ended, and the two girls heard quick steps swish away through pine needles.

"Come on, Caitlin, we need to follow."

"Dani, I don't think this a great time to approach Professor Fairburn, and besides, listen, is she…"

"Crying?" Dani finished.

Both girls leaned into the bush in an attempt to peer through the foliage and catch sight of the mysterious woman. They caught glimpses of a slim, serious woman in her mid-twenties. Since she paced back and forth, it was hard to tell for sure, but she seemed to frown a lot. The girls edged forward with painstaking effort and self-control, without so much as the snap of a twig to betray them. Until Nikki spotted a chipmunk trespassing in his forest. The dog lurched forward, pulling the leash and the two crouching twelve-year-olds off-balance. A howl shook the forest, and the girls crashed to the ground. As they struggled to rise from their stomachs, a voice somewhere overhead asked a perfectly natural question.

"Spying, which implies being quiet, with a howling beagle seems something of an oxymoron, don't you think, girls?" A smiling grown-up with tears in her eyes looked down at them.

First Caitlin, then Dani rose into a sitting position, somewhat confused and more than a little embarrassed.

Dani mumbled as she brushed leaves and twigs off her overalls. "We were just passing by, but Nikki here—" she nodded with a quiet look of disappointment "—needed to stop for a rest."

Caitlin's brow wrinkled with obvious curiosity. "What's an oxymoron?"

The woman's strained expression softened as she wiped away tears. "It's a contradiction in terms. I mean, spying on the one hand and a beagle on the other. What greater contradiction could there be?"

Caitlin's lips curled upward about as much as Dani's curled down. Suppressing her grin, Caitlin said, "My friend's been trying to train her dog. It's just that beagles don't always agree with their owners, do they, Dani?" Now even the serious lady's face folded into a smile.

"An oxymoron," Dani said thoughtfully, "is kinda what our dads might call a 'fun run.' Skinny people torturing themselves, and they call it fun?" Dani looked down at Nikki, who had abandoned chipmunk-chasing and started turning in a circle in search of the perfect snooze position. "He's a smart dog. It's just that he's smart in a way people don't understand. It's kinda like…"

"Idiosyncratic intelligence?"

The girls gaped, then said, "What?"

"Quirky, different, unconventional?"

Now Dani grinned. "Yeah, that's it! Nikki has idiosyncratic intelligence."

Caitlin rolled her eyes.

The woman shrugged.

"People just don't understand how smart Nikki is," Dani said.

"Oh, boy!" Caitlin groaned.

"Well, he'll have to be intelligent to escape being seen or heard by the warden with that howl, since dogs aren't allowed in the park," the woman said.

"Come on, Dani, tell her about Nikki's opera lessons," Caitlin urged.

Dani ignored her friend's comment. "We know, miss. It's just that we didn't find out until we arrived here at camp."

The woman held out her hand decisively. "My name is Shannon Kennedy. Call me Shannon. What's your name?"

Ouch, Caitlin thought. "Caitlin," she said, hoping her hand wasn't broken.

"I'm Dani, and I guess you've sort of met Nikki." Dani's mind was already past introductions and onto the case. "Shannon, we couldn't help overhearing you talking to Professor Fairburn."

"Of course not," Shannon agreed with a wry smile.

"And, well, we're quite interested in his research 'cause we're doing a school project."

"During your summer holidays?"

"Yes," Dani pressed on. "'Cause we're going into grade seven and there's a lot more work in junior high and—"

"And you can never start doing your homework too early," Caitlin completed in an insincere, singsong voice.

Shannon folded her arms and mimicked Caitlin's voice. "And the moon is made of Swiss cheese."

The girls looked at each other and fiddled. Dani shoved both hands deep into her overalls and pulled her pockets inside out while Caitlin nervously chewed on her braid. Nikki, alone, remained relaxed, lying on the forest floor, occasionally snorting pine needles, the only sign of life from beagle dreamland.

Shannon waited, her face solemn and expectant. Finally she let out a breath similar to Nikki's snort, and her features softened. "I'm sorry, girls. I'm kind of upset right now, as you may have been forced to overhear. I had an argument with Professor Fairburn, my academic adviser, and he'll no longer work with me." As she thought about the recent encounter, her face became serious again. "It makes me so mad. I mean, I'm only doing what I believe in." Another thought entered her mind, and the stern expression softened once more. "Say, how do you know Dustin Fairburn? You're not doing a thesis in grade seven, are you?"

Dani answered carefully. "Our dads have read some of his historical books."

"We won the Glebe Historical Society Contest," Caitlin cut in nonchalantly.

Shannon's eyes lit up. "You're the two girls who won that contest!" She placed her hands on her cheeks. "Professor Fairburn told me all about you. He was tremendously impressed, and so was I." She leaned down, as if to take the girls into her confidence. "But you know, he was really perplexed about how you two managed to come up with the right answer. He never did figure it out, but he sure did try. Ha! I loved it. The great Professor Fairburn finally stumped. That was the only time anyone ever saw him stuck for an answer." She grabbed the girls' hands and shook them again. "I'm so glad to meet you. What a coincidence."

Ouch, Caitlin thought again.

Yeah, that's it, Dani thought, *just a coincidence*.

"Your success winning the contest remains a totally unsolved mystery."

Dani beamed.

"What I would give to stump the master, just once, about anything..." Shannon's voice trailed off and her eyes moistened. She made a deep Nikki-like sigh, then continued angrily. “Even if he is the smartest person who ever lived, he can’t be right all the time. I mean, you two proved he’s fallible, human even. My research has always been guided, at least in part, by my feelings. Is that so objectionable? Intuition isn’t totally absent from historical research.” Now she was getting really upset. “I mean, none of the conventional evidence adds up. There were so many leads not followed up. There were mistakes made and assumptions that might have prevented the truth from ever coming out.” Shannon finished with arms flailing and girls ducking. “This is a mystery that’s solvable, even if Dustin Fairburn doesn’t believe in intuition.”

Dani’s attention was riveted. Caitlin admired Shannon’s pearl earrings.

Dani gulped. “And what mystery might that be?”

“The mystery of Tom Thomson’s death,” Shannon replied with surprise. “I thought you guys were listening.”

“I guess we missed some,” Dani said meekly as she dealt with the shock of Shannon’s words.

Caitlin decided to ask her about the earrings later. “Do you mean you and Dustin Fairburn were arguing about Tom Thomson?”

“And you believe,” Dani said slowly and evenly, “he was murdered, don’t you?”

Nikki inhaled mightily, scattering pine needles in a record-breaking snort as the three companions stood in heavy silence.

10

And Pierce the Deep Wood's Woven Shade

Shannon stood her ground and counted her fingers with dramatic intent. "So am I correct in assuming the situation is as follows? First, you, Caitlin, and you, Dani—" she nodded like a woodpecker drilling into a tree "—my newfound friends, are going to help me prove once and for all that the great Canadian painter Tom Thomson was murdered, thereby settling a mystery of eighty-five years. Second, you're going to help me shock Professor Fairburn, not to mention the entire art world. Third, you'll give me credit for the research we uncover so I can use it for my Ph.D. thesis. And fourth, although we'll remain lifelong friends, you can never quite reveal the source of your information for fear of upsetting my adult beliefs."

Dani threw her lucky oval stone into the air and snapped it back into her hand. "Yup."

"You'll just have to trust your intuition," Caitlin said.

Shannon took a seat on an old oak log. "Touché. I did

say that, didn't I?"

Dani pulled her overalls straps and rocked on her canvas running shoes. "We can't say how long it'll take exactly, but if you give us a couple of days, I'm sure we can come up with something."

Caitlin glanced at her friend and whispered in her ear, "Dani, how are we going to find anything?"

Dani maintained her composure as she whispered out of the side of her mouth, "I have no idea."

"Oh, good," Caitlin whispered back. "I thought I missed something."

Shannon watched the girls and folded her arms. "You're not keeping secrets from your new partner, are you, girls?"

Dani rocked. "Oh, no. We're just talking strategy."

"Oh, so you have a plan then?" Shannon asked.

"Well, not exactly…" Dani frowned as she came down from the balls of her feet.

"But we're planning to have a plan," Caitlin said cleverly.

Shannon laughed, then sighed. "I don't really expect you two to solve this mystery, but I could use some company. And I'd like to tell you about my research, what my intuition tells me. Maybe we could meet tomorrow sometime. I don't think Professor Fairburn will be very helpful any longer."

"Sure," Dani reasoned. "It would help the case for us to learn more about this Tom Thomson guy and about intuition."

Nikki suddenly rose and announced with a uniquely beagle-esque howl that he had returned to the world of the living.

"Guess we better get going," Dani said. "Otherwise our

dads will get real worried."

"And besides," Caitlin added, "we can't keep a dog, who isn't even allowed to be in the park, waiting."

"Can you find your own way back to your campsite, or would you like an adult escort?" Shannon asked.

"That's okay, Shannon," Dani said. "We'll be fine. In fact, we could find our own way back with our eyes closed."

"What would happen if we tried to find our way back with our eyes open?" Caitlin asked no one in particular.

"Well, I'm so glad we met," Shannon said, shooting out her hand to shake again.

Ouch, Caitlin thought once again, smiling nonetheless.

"I really needed some inspiration after that encounter with Professor Fairburn. Usually when I get upset I just take a run, which is most days, come to think of it—"

Dani's eyes suddenly opened wide. "We'd better go. We're real late."

"Okay…I guess," Shannon said, slightly puzzled by Dani's reaction. "My campsite's right over by that red Volkswagen, so you know where to find me."

Caitlin thought she saw more tears in Shannon's eyes as the woman waved goodbye. Then she glared at her friend. "For beagle's sake, Dani, what's the hurry?"

"Going for a run." Dani spread her hands wide and strode ahead of Caitlin, who was left to decipher this limited insight.

"So?" Caitlin finally prompted, trotting after her friend.

Dani stopped and pivoted. "So…" She waited for Caitlin to see the obvious.

Caitlin groaned. "So let's review the scene of the crime?"

"Shannon going on a run doesn't remind you of any recent detective work?"

"Whatever," Caitlin said as she threw away the twig she'd been chewing on. "Wait! Omigosh, our dads will have discovered their running shoes are missing by now!"

"And if we're away too long, we'll become the number-one suspects!"

"So what are you waiting for? Come on."

Dani opened her mouth to reply but decided to put her efforts into getting a stride ahead of her friend.

"Are you sure this is the way back to our campsite, Dani? I don't remember this trail at all."

Dani had resumed her habitual lead. "It has to be this way," Dani asserted as she dragged a compass from a pocket in her overalls and began fiddling with it. "Our dads should be directly northeast of here."

"What happened to our map?" Caitlin asked.

"I thought we'd try a more challenging way of navigating."

Caitlin's moan echoed between towering pine trees. Then a shadow descended on the girls as clouds passed in front of the sun. The pair stopped, unsure which direction to follow. Since Dani had begun navigating by compass, they hadn't seen a discernible path out of the forest. The girls listened carefully for any sound of humanity, but only the swish of whispering pines overhead could be heard in any direction.

Caitlin grumbled, Dani's stomach growled, and Nikki sniffed at someone's barbecue a couple hundred miles away. In all directions the forest seemed to end in a dark enclosure of green.

"Let's face it, Dani, we're lost."

"We're not lost. We're just geographically challenged... temporarily."

"Just like Nikki's opera voice is temporarily sounding like a howl."

Dani's face registered the frustration and annoyance of a seasoned detective momentarily stumped. "Over there! It looks like a path opening up."

Caitlin scrutinized layers of green, deeper green, and deepest green. "I'm sorry, Dani, but I can't quite see the sidewalk signs."

Dani ignored her friend. "There. Over there. You can't expect to see it easily. You have to train yourself to notice the smallest details."

"Uh-huh." Caitlin turned in a complete circle, fearing what her friend might say next.

"Come on, Caitlin, let's try it. According to my compass, this should be the right way."

The threesome continued deeper into the forest, with Dani leading, compass in hand, Nikki sniffing left and right, and Caitlin walking backward, searching for a way back.

Dani was puzzled. The opening that had seemed a likely path had disappeared completely.

Nikki was enjoying the smorgasbord of forest scents but was confused by his master's stop-and-start pace of travel. Every time they stopped and he began to look for perfect snooze quarters, a tug on the leash signalled it was time to move on. Caitlin managed to continue walking backward on a difficult trail, checking over her shoulder every few seconds and vaguely wondering how long it would take to walk backward all the way home to Ottawa.

Nikki and the girls shuffled along in a sad-looking line

for about ten minutes. Natural forest sounds swirled around: wind swishing through trees, dog sniffing distant hamburgers, and friends grunting as they frequently bumped into each other. Otherwise the forest was very, very quiet. As the girls penetrated deeper into darkening shades of green, the wind disappeared, the sniffing subsided, and only occasional grunting interrupted the silence. Finally an exasperated noise thundered from Dani. “Why the heck can’t we find the way back?” Her face was totally misshapen by detective angst.

“Now I know why crabs don’t live in the forest,” Caitlin mumbled as she stumbled backward into her friend again. Caitlin grabbed at a pine branch to steady herself. To her surprise, the branch wasn’t connected to a tree. She reached for a second branch, then stood holding a pine limb in each hand.

“Do you mind?” an agitated voice demanded, piercing the deep wood’s woven shade.

The girls crashed into each other’s backside as Nikki reared up and expressed his beagle nature. Branches stirred behind a makeshift pine enclosure as the voice continued. “Isn’t it enough that I find my own place, not bothering anyone, far away from the madding crowd, and even so I have to put up with city rumblings, destruction… and a dog?”

A sour face with haggard, weepy eyes, long, matted hair, and a thick grey beard stared out from under pine boughs. The girls clung to each other as Nikki wound his leash around their legs.

“They’re not allowed here, you know.”

Dani and Caitlin glanced at each other, noses touching

and vision blurred, pinned together by Nikki's leash. They turned their heads back toward the old man and responded with a nervous "We know."

The old man crawled out of a hovel on his hands and knees. "You see, I don't like company. I can't stand loud noise." Nikki naturally took this as a cue to release his loudest, longest beagle howl of all time.

The kooky old man covered his ears and bit his lip as he raised himself to a shaky standing position. For a few moments he looked as if he might topple. He attempted to steady himself by holding a branch but ended up clutching a pine bough that was part of his shelter.

"Touché," Caitlin said in a high-pitched voice.

"Caitlin!" Dani protested as she struggled with Nikki's leash. "He might be dangerous…and we can't exactly run away yet 'cause—"

"We're tied up at the moment," Caitlin finished with a nervous grin.

"This is no joking matter," Dani continued as Nikki, freed from the girls' legs, began barking at the old man, who gently placed the pine bough back in its place, covered his ears, and waited for Nikki's serenade to end.

"Dani," Caitlin said as a sudden thought occurred to her, "maybe this is the scary hermit our dads were talking about."

Although stooped and unsteady on his feet, the old man towered above the girls. The shredded ruins of a tweed suit hung from his long, bony limbs. What looked like an old rope dangled from his scrawny neck by a perfect Windsor knot. With his dishevelled, dirty hair covered with leaves and his arms raised to protect his ears, he was a perfect scarecrow.

Nikki's attention had meanwhile switched to an interesting odour from the old man's shelter. As he clawed his way toward the object of his desire, the old man lowered his arms, scratched at various parts of his body, and declared, "They sent the hounds to sniff me out, did they?"

The girls looked at each other, this time from a reasonable distance. "They?"

"Ah, so you admit to the scheme to capture me but are attempting to protect the perpetrators!"

"What?"

His sinewy finger stood in the air like driftwood in water. "What could be more obvious than your pack of killing beasts and hunting party of thousands?" The indignation in his eyes was short-lived as he peered at the girls standing small and silent. Once again the finger rose and the expression returned, but then he wavered and, being worn out, stopped. He tilted toward the girls, cupped his mouth with his hands, and asked in a little boy's voice, "Say, would anyone in your hunting party happen to have a chocolate bar?"

Dani plucked half a Mint Royale from her overalls and thrust it in the direction of the old man. Each approached the other with slow, tentative steps, like two soldiers on a battlefield exchanging terms of a truce. A scattering of teeth in various stages of decay formed a jagged line inside the old man's crooked grin. As he chewed the chocolate bar, he backpedalled into his shelter and rummaged through its contents for several minutes.

"What should we do?" Caitlin whispered.

Before Dani could answer, the great apparition unfolded from the hovel, carrying a clump of decaying matter. As the girls' faces performed contortions of disgust, the old man proudly brandished his prize, then dropped it to the delight of Nikki. While Dani debated lunging forward to protect her dog, the old man calmly announced, "Bone for the hound. It'll keep him from eating me." Then he shifted his own bones into a kneeling position and patted Nikki, who received the attention with energetic tail swishes.

Despite a certain amount of fear, the girls couldn't help being curious. "Um, mister..." Dani began, stroking her chin.

"Do you really live in that...that thing?" Caitlin finished.

The old man continued lavishing attention on the willing killer hound. His grin melted like a Mint Royale, and he became thoughtful as he turned his attention to the human world. "I'm sure seasoned bounty hunters such as yourselves have read my résumé."

"Huh?" Dani and Caitlin said in unison.

"Yes, it's true. There's no point in gloating. Still, the capture of terrible criminals has always bestowed a certain notoriety. That I can't deny." The old man squinted one eye and stroked his whiskers. "I suppose the criminal and the lawmaker, the pursued and the pursuer, have always been of the same spirit in some respects."

"Huh?" both girls exclaimed again.

Looking clearly at the girls for the first time, the old man slowly raised his arms, exhaled air from his lungs, and said with resignation, "I won't resist. You've won. You can now drag me through town in shackles, for I confess."

"Confess what?" Dani asked.

"I, Nathaniel Peabody Longfellow, am guilty. I murdered the famous painter Tom Thomson."

11
A Tall Tale

Caitlin's braid and some saliva unceremoniously flew out of her mouth. After a moment's hesitation, her face wrinkled as she said, "Wow! We sure solved that mystery fast." Turning to her still-shocked friend, she asked, "Dani, just how did we do that, anyway?"

A pesky fly flew into Dani's mouth before she realized it was hanging open.

Longfellow lifted a finger and pointed. "It would appear your tonsils have a visitor."

Dani made a face as she spat out the fly and ended up with saliva dripping down her chin. Both girls wiped their faces with the backs of their hands, then realized that was only a partial solution and continued wiping their hands on their pants. Dani struggled to formulate a question. "How…why…is it possible?"

Longfellow extended his long, lean limbs in a gesture of surrender. "Oh, it's true, all right. It is I, and only I, who murdered Tom Thomson, or worse, so take me away. Do you think you could manage to get me a quiet cell where people won't gawk? Would a daily ration of chocolate be asking too much? And, if I do say so, your selection was mighty tasty."

"What could be worse than murder, Mr. Longfellow?" Caitlin asked.

The hermit's long left arm arched back to his face where he delicately and deliberately scratched his long nose. "Surely bounty hunters like yourselves must be aware of the full extent of my crimes."

"Yes, of course," Dani said, rising on her toes and gripping the straps of her overalls.

"Huh?" Caitlin said, thinking what a crime it would be to miss dinner.

"Please tell us more, Mr. Longfellow," Dani continued, raising an eyebrow to silence her friend.

"I murdered Tom Thomson and diminished his reputation as a painter." The hermit paused, but not for long. "All an accident, of course."

"The murder was an accident?" Dani asked.

"Well, in a manner of speaking, that is, losing those sketches...and that other thing."

Dani no longer pulled on her straps and her running shoes were firmly anchored to the forest floor. "Sketches? That other thing?"

"Six sketches to be exact, but naturally you knew that. I suppose the diary was less important. Still, it's inexcusable for a curator to lose holdings."

"Did you say 'diary'?" Dani asked slowly and clearly.

"Oh, come now, why play so coy? I did it, and now I

must pay the piper. Give me shackles or solitude!"

Caitlin was growing increasingly annoyed. "For beagle's sake, what's going on?"

Longfellow scratched himself and thought about Caitlin's question. "You fellows really don't know about my sordid past?"

"Not a thing," Caitlin answered.

"You're not here to arrest me then?"

"Nope," Dani said. "But we are…"

"Lost," Caitlin finished.

"We're real interested in your story, though," Dani added.

"Well, I don't know. I—"

"Chocolate bars," Dani said temptingly.

Longfellow rubbed his long fingers together. "I suppose I could show you the way to the trading post. I go there sometimes."

"For chocolate?" Caitlin coaxed.

"That's right. One of the young men working outside obliges and spares me the hardship of going inside among all those people." Longfellow made a face of disgust. "Come on, fellows, this way."

Dani hesitated, unsure if they should follow this strange, and very long, Longfellow. But with a murder mystery unsolved and the truth about Tom Thomson hanging in the balance, she barrelled headlong into double trouble. "Well, I guess it's okay, mister."

The mysteries of the forest surrounded the odd group as they set out. Green ferns gently brushed their shins as they made their way toward the path. Green pines and spruce trees swayed soothingly over the girls' heads and under Longfellow's ears as they meandered across the forest floor. Green tree limbs heaved and groaned far over even Longfellow's ears, forming a compete canopy, except where shafts of sunlight refracted light to the forest floor, like a smash and stab of passion on canvas.

Dani took great strides to keep up with Longfellow's long, creaking gait. Caitlin skipped along behind. "So, Mr. Longfellow, sir, did you really kill Tom Thomson?"

Longfellow stopped dead in his tracks. "What? You crazy? Of course, I didn't kill him. Heck, I'd have to have been about a hundred if I did. I'm only sixty-seven. Well, I will be soon. It's still August, isn't it? Yes? Good. You see, what happened was that I…shall we say…burned out, retirement and all, and I never did recover from losing that pesky diary—"

"What diary?" Dani interjected. Then she said more softly, "Mr. Longfellow, sir?"

"Well, let me think. About twenty years ago or more someone tried to sell his father's diary to the McMichael Canadian Art Collection in Kleinburg, of which I was curator. A fellow by the name of Deschamps, I think. A rather angry fellow, I must gingerly add. Of course, he may have had some reason to be angry."

"Look, a trail!" Caitlin shouted. "Maybe we won't die of cold and hunger and without a washroom, after all."

"And would you have any idea where we might be able to locate this angry Mr. Deschamps, Mr. Longfellow?" Dani asked, paying no attention to Caitlin's outburst.

"Well, we didn't exactly keep in touch." Longfellow's voice quavered as he wobbled down a steep incline toward the waiting trail. "But, yes, he's likely still in Huntsville, complaining bitterly to all who'll listen about my career-ending mistake."

Dani huffed with excitement as well as from the effort of keeping up with Longfellow's long strides. "Mr. Longfellow, just how did you lose this diary and Tom Thomson's sketches?"

Longfellow seemed not to hear the question, or else he ignored it. But just as Dani puffed up to ask it again, the old man stopped, put his long finger to his long chin, and surveyed the forest with no particular object in his view. With a hollow look he pointed a long, crooked finger down a long, crooked trail and said, "That way." And then, slowly turning back toward the path and his hovel, he added, "Burnt them to ash."

12
The Secret of Chaos Theory

Three wretched and hungry companions neared the campsite as the late-afternoon sun waned and barbecues drenched the forest in pungent aromas. Nikki pulled on his leash with excitement. Dani held her hungry hound with both arms extended, looking more like a water-skier on the lake than a land-loving detective. Caitlin's thoughts vacillated between barbecues and outhouses.

"Dani, I don't know what the heck we can do about Tom Thomson's murder. Mr. Longfellow said the diary we're looking for is gone forever, and it's not as if they grow on trees." Caitlin held her hands upward as if to demonstrate the sense of her words, but paused as she gazed into the shafts of sunlight sifting through gently swaying branches. "Of course, diaries are written on paper, which does grow on trees…"

Dani's determined pace didn't slacken even with the campsite in sight. "The way I see it, we have two choices."

Dani fastened Nikki's leash to her overalls and slammed her fist into her palm, indicating her singular desire to limit the choices to one.

Caitlin sighed. "I just knew this was coming."

"Either we give up and tell Tom Thomson we don't have a clue about how to prove to the world he was murdered—"

"Which he was."

"I'm not finished yet. Or we go to Huntsville to see this Deschamps character. Of course, we need to find out more about potential suspects in this case, especially if they're known to keep a diary. I mean, we can't be sure what Mr. Longfellow said about burning the diary. I wonder if Dad could take us to Huntsville—wherever that is—but, then again, how do we explain why we need to talk to this guy about— No, our dads wouldn't like that. And we should go back to Tom Thomson's campsite and see if we can get some more clues. Hey, maybe Shannon can take us to Huntsville. Well, Caitlin, which choice should we make?" Dani didn't wait for an answer but continued puzzling over strategies and possibilities.

Caitlin sighed once more, this time with resignation, and muttered to herself, "Onward, oh, Captain. Tallyho!"

Dani finished her complicated calculations. "The way I see it, we have one choice."

Being two hours late, the girls expected to be overwhelmed by fatherly questions. But campsite commotion featured hot discussion that deflected hot questions from the two aspiring detectives.

"Both of us, both pairs!" Dani's dad frantically fumed.

"Which is two too many times to be a coincidence!" Caitlin's dad added.

For several minutes the girls waited patiently, arms folded, pretending to look sympathetic while the dads continued their tirade. Finally, when all facts and speculations had been said and said again, Bob simply asked, "Just who would do such a thing?"

With this burning question, the two skinny dads briefly scrutinized their naked feet but found nothing suspicious there. Their eyes then turned to their daughters. John scratched his tense jaw. "Yes, who?"

"Who indeed?" Bob echoed, rubbing a muscle in his leg, stiff no doubt from lack of exercise.

At that point Nikki's brilliance for well-timed howls reasserted itself. All eyes became riveted on the detached detectives turned prime suspects. Nikki bellowed again, this time with some feeling, as the dads' eyebrows slowly arched into menacing accusations.

"Well, girls," John began, "do you happen to know anything about..." He paused, reluctant to accuse such young, innocent girls.

"Our missing running shoes?" Bob finished without any hesitation whatsoever.

Happily fate intervened to deliver the girls out of the frying pan, but unfortunately into the fire.

"Oh, no, that truck. It's the warden again," Dani said.

Nikki protested only mildly at being pulled through the forest and away from the sizzling barbecue at the speed of smell. As Dani passed a campsite garbage can, Nikki's attention became fixed on a half-eaten bag of popcorn. While Dani struggled to control her popcorn-loving canine, a light bulb went on in her head and she knew Nikki had found the solution to his own noise-pollution problem. Five minutes later Dani was casually strolling back to the campsite, leaving Nikki happily munching on lightly buttered, salt-free popcorn.

"By the time he realizes he's tied to the tree," Dani reasoned to herself, "the warden should be long gone."

Dani arrived back at the campsite in time to hear Warden Willins switch from the mystery of that "dang howlin' hound" to the mystery of that "horrible hermit." The warden yanked his trousers up to no avail and sucked on the ends of his moustache while he listened to yet another mystery, this time about stolen shoes.

"And you say yer runnin' shoes are missin'?" The warden liked to ask questions about stated facts, just to be sure folks were on the up-and-up. Satisfied the skinny men were levelling with him, he momentarily veered off-course. "Now I know I shouldn't give advice during an important case, but you seem in a bad way standin' there."

The two dads shifted uneasily.

"Tell ya what I'm gonna do. If my investigation doesn't turn up yer shoes, I know just the place where you can get the best fish an' tackle gear round these parts. It's down Huntsville way."

John and Bob were unsure where they stood, but stood speechless nonetheless.

The warden squinted one eye and continued. "Of course, they also have them fancy runnin' gizmos fer your feet."

Finally comprehending, the dads smiled.

"Tell 'em Willins sent ya. Wouldn't be surprised if youse get a five-percent discount."

John and Bob nodded.

The warden became serious. "These sightings, crimes, look bad. We can't jump to conclusions, but this just fits a pattern, doesn't it? He's getttin' bolder and bolder. Next he'll be runnin' off with yer young'uns—if you're not careful.

He held up his hands dramatically. "Don't mean to alarm, just concerned, is all." The warden leaned toward the dads, half whispering as he asked if it was okay to talk in front of the womenfolk. The dads nodded, and the warden continued, cracking his stubby fingers as he spoke. "Well, folks, lemme say that after investigatin' the matter at hand..." The warden paused to investigate his own hand. Satisfied, he continued. "I now have positive proof this here hermit critter exists, all right." He puffed out his cheeks to cap off his announcement.

"But, Warden, we already told you the hermit exists!" John protested.

"Yesiree, my investigation was intended to confirm or disprove your allegations."

Caitlin wondered if that was steam coming out of Dani's father's ears or simply humidity.

Bob intervened before his friend created an incident. "So, Warden Willins, is that the extent of your…investigation?"

"Nosiree," the warden thundered, heaving up his trousers. "This here hermit has been sighted again, half-crazed, threatenin' like, not too far from the Portage Store itself. So he just might be gettin' desperate…" The group waited for the habitual belt tug before the man continued. "So I came here today to advise you to be careful, stick together, and watch yer young'uns."

Caitlin half yawned and let the words she'd been chewing

on slip from her mouth. "Oh, him, yeah, Dani and I met him today. He's kinda weird, but nice enough in his own way."

Dani tensed as Caitlin dropped this bombshell. Still, she followed on cue. "Really quite harmless, actually. You know, like a loud dog that's really kinda cuddly." Dani shrugged and giggled, immediately regretting her own example of harmlessness.

Caitlin thought Dani was rather clever. "Yeah, you know how dogs bark sometimes and scare people, and some dogs howl and really scare people."

Dani's forehead wrinkled like an old baboon's. "Caitlin," she cautioned. But her friend was too busy grinning at the group standing in front of them with their mouths hanging open in disbelief.

"Well, now, young lady," Warden Willins said, both hands on his belt, rocking slowly on his heels, preparing his line of questioning. "Are you just tryin' to be grown-up here, young missy?"

"No." Both girls calmly shook their heads.

"Well, I…" the warden began without knowing where to take things.

"Did you really see this man, Dani?" John asked frantically. "You could have been killed!"

"Caitlin, what in the world were you thinking?" Bob asked his daughter.

About getting back here, Caitlin thought.

"It was okay, Dad," Dani said. "He's kinda scary to look at, but he's not going to hurt anyone."

"I'll be the judge of that, young lady," the warden harrumphed.

"I'm sure he wouldn't hurt a flea. In fact, he's afraid of people—all people. Dad, I think he might need help."

The warden squinted. "If you two misses saw him, tell us where he lives."

"We don't know," Caitlin answered. "We just ran into him when we were lost."

"Yeah, Dad, then he brought us back to the Portage Store."

Warden Willins's mouth lay on his chest like a dead raccoon on the highway.

John fumbled with the obvious. "Are you girls saying…I mean, are you really telling us this hermit character actually led you two back to safety?"

Just then all eyes became glued to a wild beast running in full flight, no doubt pursuing big game and small squirrels through the jungle. Nikki had bounded through the campsite, leash in tow, toward barbecue fumes several campsites away.

Nobody had time to react as the dog passed between Caitlin and Dani, between the dads, and right between the wobbly legs of Clayton Worther Willins, warden of Algonquin Park. Seconds that seemed like hours passed before anyone could summon the presence of mind to react. And then the campsite erupted into chaos. People ran, yelled, and bumped into one another as they scampered after the fugitive hound. The warden attempted, in vain, to direct scurrying bodies toward a systematic and successful capture. Unfortunately for the lawmaker, the other adults also tried to direct the group activity. The girls added to the confusion by yelling and running just for the heck of it. As the shouting subsided into debate about who should do what, the girls tumbled to the grass, giggling.

"This is perfect," Dani whispered, pulling grass out of her mouth.

"And kind of fun, too," Caitlin added, helping her friend up by the straps of her overalls.

"Come on," Dani said, "let's grab a wiener, our secret weapon for catching wild animals."

Meanwhile the warden huffed and puffed for about two hundred yards, pulling his pants up more than once. "Dang," he managed to spit between laboured breaths. With one more gigantic and determined tug of his belt, placing his pants high over his stomach, he tottered awkwardly to his truck. Once in, he thundered over potholed roads, leaving dust to settle on barbecues for miles in every direction.

Nikki lifted his head as the truck passed by, smacking his lips, enjoying the remnants of the warden's ham sandwich. The park official had left the window open on the passenger side of his truck, and Nikki had reasoned that lightly buttered, salt-free popcorn really wasn't enough to satisfy an outdoor dog at dinnertime. He might have been caught inhaling the incriminating evidence when the warden got back into his truck, but the vehicle was hot and the shade under the oak tree nearby was a much more inviting location to eat. Besides, if he had stayed in the truck, he would have missed the lovely wiener his master offered him two minutes later. Life sure could be sweet.

13

Running into Trouble

By 8:30 the next morning the girls and their dads were rumbling down Highway 60 toward Huntsville.

"Don't know, John. Sure, New Balance has the antipronation bars, but Nike has air gel for reduced weight-bearing stress, especially on pavement," Bob reasoned.

"But, Bob, variable-width sizing must appeal to you in particular," John countered.

"True, and a good point, but I find that Adidas fit just, as well."

"Really?"

The girls looked at each other and mimed a series of *blah, blah, blahs*, not for the first time.

"If only you could get one shoe with gel, antipronation features, and variable-width sizing," John summarized.

Nikki lifted his head from his cozy curled position and licked the air-gel antipronation pad on his left paw. Exhausted by the exercise, he yawned and went back to sleep.

"Yeah, right," Bob answered, overcome by the good sense of it all.

"And a partridge in a pear tree," Caitlin whispered rather loudly. Fortunately the dads had air gel in their ears and didn't hear.

"Next stop, Huntsville," John called out like a conductor to amuse the girls. Caitlin and Dani rolled their eyes.

"Are we there *yet*, Dad?" Dani asked.

"Over there, John. He's just leaving." Bob had spied a parking spot right in front of Huntsville Sport.

As soon as the van was parked, the men jumped out, giddy with excitement. They paced in front of the store in their sandals and shorts. Reluctantly the girls followed, having endured many running-shoe try-ons in the past. Just as Dani was about to suggest they meet their dads after all the shoes in the store had been sampled, say, in about three weeks, a flurry of exclamations erupted.

"It just can't be!"

"Closed. How can it be closed?"

"The sign says it's closed 'cause of the summer regatta," Caitlin said.

"It'll be open tomorrow," Dani offered.

Having vented a few choice words, the two dads stood speechless. As the girls attempted to help their helpless dads through the present crisis, they heard a polite introductory cough.

"Shannon!" The girls' excitement at seeing their friend equalled their dads' disappointment at their lot in life.

"Dad, this is Shannon Kennedy," both girls said in unison. Their dads nodded hello, but remained preoccupied.

"Shannon, are you here doing *research* today?" Dani

stressed the word *research* and winked at Shannon so as to be understood.

"No, actually, I was going to shop for moose at the library..."

Dani placed her foot on Shannon's foot to be noticed, and winked so hard that Caitlin wondered if her left eye would ever open again.

"Oh, well, um, the fact is, although I haven't done any research yet today, I intend to spend the rest of the day in scholarly pursuit. Would you two girls care to join me?"

Dani's expression registered complete affirmation.

"I'll be mainly just reading old letters and looking at old photos in the Huntsville library, and you might be pretty bored."

"Oh, no!" Dani nearly shouted.

"But it's such a beautiful day and you girls are on your holiday," Shannon said mischievously.

Dani's hands were extended outward, as if Nikki were pulling on the leash. "No, really, we don't care about the day. I mean, it's more important to learn about research stuff...for when we go to university, you know..." Her voice trailed off without conviction.

"And besides, we really like being bored on beautiful days," Caitlin chirped, but her expression changed as she reflected on what she had just said.

Shannon decided to end the torture. "I'm a Ph.D. student in history," she said to the dads, who were standing in their shorts and sandals, confused and disappointed, all dressed up with no place to run. "I'd be happy to instruct the girls in proper research methods."

Both dads stood stunned, witless, and shoeless.

"I'm staying at a campsite on Canoe Lake, so I can have the girls back in time for supper."

"Um," John finally ventured.

"Dad?" Dani cried, attempting to break through her father's running-shoe stupor.

"Oh, yeah, sure, research..." John mumbled.

"Preparation for university—sounds fine, I guess," Bob added.

"Well, goodbye," Dani abruptly said, pulling Caitlin and Shannon by their arms.

"Dani, make sure the cellphone is turned on," John called after them in a dispirited voice.

The threesome glanced over their shoulders and caught glimpses of the two confused skinny men still standing at the entrance to the shoe store.

"Do you think they'll leave today?" Dani asked.

"It depends," Shannon answered with a smile, "whether or not they do a Ph.D. thesis to try to figure out what could motivate their twelve-year-old daughters to spend a summer doing advanced homework. What have you two done to those poor men? They look as if they've seen a ghost."

Caitlin paused mid-stride, a deep frown on her face. "Maybe we should be worried, too. Come to think of it, schoolwork in the summer doesn't sound natural."

The girls looked at each other, half smiling, half gulping.

"It's a long story," Caitlin began. "Kinda like a Ph.D. thesis."

"And we have work to do," Dani added, now determined and racing ahead of her friends like a beagle on the hunt.

"Mind if I tag along?" Shannon asked.

"We kinda hoped you would," Dani said.

"Unless, of course, you make us run to where we have to go," Caitlin contributed archly.

"I have a feeling the only thing I'll run into with you two," Shannon said with a sly smile, "is trouble."

An hour later the three friends and a friendly beagle stood in front of a dilapidated shack.

"This is the address," Dani said, checking and rechecking what she'd written down from the Huntsville phone book.

Shannon was obviously puzzled. "But, girls, I still don't understand."

"Remember our deal—no questions," Dani reminded her new friend. "We have some information from an unidentified source, and sometimes you have to believe in intuition."

"We could just leave a note," Caitlin offered, glancing around nervously.

Dani's eyebrow rose, indicating annoyance with her fellow detective.

"Should you knock, or me, or you maybe?" Caitlin suggested, chewing on her braid as if she were starving.

Dani puffed up her cheeks, steadied herself, and resolved to proceed without knowing how, what, or why.

"Perhaps we shouldn't, Dani..." Shannon began. But it was too late, for Dani had boldly stepped forward and rapped her knuckles on a rickety old wooden door. There was no answer.

Dani inhaled deeply and rapped again.

This time the silence was interrupted by a high-pitched voice behind them. "What youse lookin' for?"

Shannon and the girls spun to greet the voice. But the surprise of the voice was nothing compared to the shock of seeing an old woman in their path holding a headless human, dripping with fresh red blood.

14
The Mystery of Tom Turkey

Well, at least it appeared to be a headless human…until the three companions stopped screaming long enough to look again. Nikki howled and wagged his tail, pleased his human friends finally understood how to express themselves. The old woman stood wiping one hand on her bloody coveralls. In her other, she held up a dripping, headless turkey carcass.

"Tarnation! G'day, girls. Come now, state yer business. Haven't got all day, you know."

First Shannon, then Caitlin, and finally Dani composed herself enough to giggle at the decomposing bird that had ruffled a few feathers.

"Oh, that." A slight smile broke across the old woman's dry, thin lips. "Just killed and plucked him. Put up quite a fight, too. Ran round the yard fer three minutes without a head till he dropped, Tom did. And that's a fact."

Caitlin and Dani chuckled. When the old woman glared

at them, the girls became serious again.

"Sorry," Caitlin said, glancing at the turkey carcass. "Lost my head for a minute."

Dani rolled her eyes. "We're sorry to disturb you, Mrs...."

"Nope, I'm no Mrs."

"That is, I mean, Ms...."

"What the dickens is a *miz*? Name's O'Brien, Wilma O'Brien."

"Oh," Dani said, rubbing her chin and looking around. "I guess we don't have the right address."

"Tom's getting heavy," the old woman said, dropping the dripping turkey onto the grass. A swarm of flies immediately buzzed around the headless bird.

Nikki sniffed a greeting and attempted to exchange pleasantries with his new friend, Tom.

"Who ya lookin' fer, honey?"

"A guy by the name of Armand Deschamps," Caitlin enunciated carefully, never taking her eyes off the lifeless bird.

"Oh, him," the old woman snorted. "Left years ago, and good riddance, too. Deadbeat he was. Changed my name then back to what it was fifty years ago."

Dani looked painfully puzzled. "Well, Wilma O'Brien, the thing is, we, that is, my friends Shannon and Caitlin, are...and, oh, my name's Dani, by the way... We kinda wondered if Mr. Deschamps—"

"Deadbeat."

"Oh, well, then—"

"Wilma, did Mr. Deadbeat ever have a really old diary by any chance?" Caitlin cut in.

The old woman glared first at Caitlin, then at Dani, and

finally at Shannon. Her eyes narrowed, cold with suspicion. "Why that lazy son of a—"

"Deadbeat," Caitlin offered.

"Couldn't hardly read, let alone write. Still," she continued, softening, "he did talk about his daddy's diary sometimes. I never read it myself, but I know'd it had an old leather cover. Seemed to think it was real important for some reason. Course, he was so full of it. If he said it was important, more 'n likely it was worth nothin' at all."

"Wilma," Dani asked slowly and deliberately, "would you have any idea where, um, Mr. Deadbeat or the diary are today?"

Wilma was about to dismiss the question altogether, but as the word *no* formed on her lips, she took in the three pleading faces and nodding heads.

"It's *really* important," Dani emphasized.

"Well," the old woman began, "guess he did say once that a fella down at the Huntsville Chamber of Commerce might be interested in buying the flea-bitten old thing."

The three friends drew breaths in unison at this revelation.

"But I dunno if the deadbeat ever did sell the darn thing, or what that fella's name was."

"Thank you, Wilma," Dani said, spontaneously reaching out to shake the old woman's hand.

Wilma peered at her hand covered in blood as Dani pulled her own hand away. The old woman bent over and wiped her fingers on the grass, then laughed for the first time. "Oh, gracious! Guess Tom's been paintin' again." She continued chuckling as she carried Tom into a shed.

"Did you see her hand?" Caitlin asked. "Tom's red blood on the green grass. The colour of a 7-Eleven store, just like your dad said, Dani."

But Dani was already moving full-steam ahead to Shannon's car. Besides, she had to work extra hard to keep a stride in front of the group, since Shannon was probably the fastest walker who ever lived. Dani and Shannon moved along at breakneck speed deep in silent thought. Caitlin skipped along in their dust, thinking that all this effort would be worth it when they spotted a 7-Eleven with ice cream. All in all, the trio walked away from the O'Brien house not quite sure if they should feel encouraged, bemused, or simply confused.

15
Hunting in Huntsville

Dani and Caitlin stood on either side of Shannon, directly in front of the desk of Mr. Percy Seymour Kent, president of the Huntsville/Lake of Bays Chamber of Commerce.

"Yes?" a high-pitched nasal voice announced more than asked.

"Well, um," Dani began, "it seems we, that is, myself and my associates Shannon and Caitlin, would like to know if you, that is..." Dani coughed, indicating momentary muddled-mind syndrome.

"Do you have Armand Deschamps's diary?" Caitlin asked bluntly, smacking her gum.

Kent's nervous eyes darted from Caitlin to Dani to Shannon and back to Caitlin. His bald scalp was oily, his face was flushed and sweaty, and his expression registered profound annoyance at the present company.

"I am sure, young lady," he said, pinching his nose as if this gesture would make the three pests go away, "I have no idea in the world what you're talking about."

Dani placed her hands on his desk for emphasis. "Sure you do, mister. It's a diary with important stuff in it about Tom Thomson."

"Indeed," the officious Kent replied, "but again I reiterate, I have no idea what you're talking about." Three faces deflated as Kent inflated his lungs with enough air to continue. "Mr. Deschamps never did give, or rather, sell, his father's diary to our Chamber of Commerce." Kent paused, eyes tilted upward, seeking strength from a higher power in dealing with trivial matters. "Because the chamber in its wisdom, and with my guidance, was unwilling to pay the price he demanded, Mr. Deschamps decided to seek greener pastures and paycheques."

A smug smile curled across Kent's lips at his clever use of the word *green*. A moment later the smile disappeared. "I believe he intended to bring the document in question to the McMichael Collection in Kleinburg, though I suspect they were equally reluctant to pay for his literary treasure." Kent's mouth twitched as he looked at Dani's hands on his desk. "Now, if you'll excuse me, I have an important committee to prepare for."

"Thanks, mister," Dani said.

"It's been a pleasure," Shannon contributed with a hint of sarcasm.

The sleuths walked down Main Street deep in thought. Sport-utility vehicles pulled motorboats and trailers through the town in search of a quiet, unspoiled lake to make noise on and spoil. And across the street two skinny men continued their search for a sports store open during the regatta.

Dani exhaled. "Poor Dad."

"Now what?" Caitlin asked as she looked around for an open ice-cream parlour.

"Well, we really should follow up with the McMichael lead," Shannon said. "I'll go to Kleinburg this afternoon. I've been meaning to do some research there, anyway."

"Which leaves us," Caitlin said, spotting a likely ice-cream place, "exactly nowhere."

"Maybe," Dani said, stroking her chin, threatening to wear through the skin. Turning to Caitlin, she whispered, "But I have a feeling Tom can help us here."

"Tom!" Caitlin exclaimed. "A dead turkey?"

"Tom Thomson," Dani said louder than she wanted to.

Caitlin looked thoughtful. "Oh, yeah."

Shannon smiled and glanced at her watch. "Of course, Tom can help. Anything you say. Girls, do you think you could call your dads and arrange to get back to your campsite with them?"

"Sure."

Good, because if I hope to talk to anyone at the gallery today who might have information about Deschamps's diary, I'll have to leave right away. Will my fellow detectives be okay?"

"Since it looks as if all the running-shoe stores are closed today, I'm sure we'll be back in Huntsville first thing tomorrow morning," Dani said.

"Why don't we meet here around 10:00 a.m. tomorrow?" Shannon suggested.

"Don't worry about us," Dani assured Shannon. "Our dads are bound to drive us back to our campsite if they *ever* give up looking for an open running-shoe store today."

"That's a big *if*," Caitlin added.

"Don't do anything I wouldn't do." Shannon glanced at her watch again and hurried on, as adults tend to do.

Caitlin and Dani wandered aimlessly down Main Street, unsure of their next move.

"We could talk to Tom again," Dani said with enthusiasm.

"Yes, we could," Caitlin agreed flatly.

"He might be able to give us another clue."

"Yes, he might."

"Guess we don't know what the heck to do next, do we?" Dani said flatly.

"That's for sure!" Caitlin said with enthusiasm.

Dani looked annoyed and frustrated. "All we know is the name of one person who hasn't been seen for years and might even be dead."

"Deschamps!" Caitlin said rather loudly and with enthusiasm.

"Shhh," Dani whispered.

An old woman striding toward the bank with her head down turned sharply and stared squarely at the girls. "Deschamps? Armand Deschamps?"

Both girls glanced back in complete bewilderment.

"Well? Well?" the little woman with birdlike features pecked away at the girls.

"Yes."

"Well, he hasn't been seen for some time now, but he had a sidekick, fellow by the name of O'Rourke, Razor O'Rourke. Works sometimes, drinks always, down at the Madill Church at old Gun Club Road and Muskoka. You might try there *with your parents*, if you really need to talk to the likes of him."

The old woman examined the girls and stressed her last words. "I won't ask why in the world you're looking for that character." But she searched with penetrating eyes nonetheless. Finally she refocused her birdlike eyes and, with quick little steps, regained her momentum toward the bank.

"Wow!" Dani said, scratching her head.

"Too bad we can't go see this guy with our parents but, oh, well, let's go home,"

Caitlin urged.

Determination gathered in Dani's features, and Caitlin groaned in anticipation of her friend's next words.

"Caitlin, this is an important lead in the case. We have to follow it up."

Dani smashed her fist into the palm of her hand, and Caitlin groaned once more as if *she* were that palm.

"Dani, you heard the lady. And besides, how can we even get there without Shannon to drive?" Caitlin frantically searched Main Street for a public washroom just in case they ended up lost in the forest again. At that moment the bird lady hurried past Dani.

"Excuse me, madam," Dani said, uncertain of her approach. The old woman stopped three strides past Dani and pivoted stiffly. "Uh…I…that is, we just wondered if you know the route to the Madill…and, um, how far it might be?"

The woman's birdlike beak went up and down as if she were a robin feeding its young. "It's on the other side of the highway, about three miles away. Why, even for a walker such as myself, it would take an hour. But I dare say you wouldn't think of walking there by yourselves, now would you?"

Dani flinched under the scrutiny of the woman's intense stare.

"No, madam," Caitlin said matter-of-factly. "She wouldn't think about it for a second."

"Well, now, I should think not!" Her beak veered at each girl before hurrying on its way.

"Wow!" Dani said thoughtfully. "I really didn't want to tell her a lie."

"I know," Caitlin said evenly, "but the truth is, you're not going to think about it even for a second, 'cause you're going to just do it." She let out a big breath of air. "And I guess I am, too."

"Hey," Dani said, pulling one of Caitlin's perfect braids, "now that's thinking!"

16

Close Encounters of the Weird Kind

An hour later the girls stood hot and sweaty under the shade of an elegant white pine. Nikki's tongue hung out the side of his mouth like one of Tom Thomson's fine lake trout. Cicadas pierced the late-afternoon silence as the girls fanned themselves and read the sign.

"Yup. This it is," Dani announced.

"Looks like we found it, all right," Caitlin added. *Now what the heck do we do?* she added in her thoughts.

Dani rubbed her hands together with excitement. "Madill is the oldest log church in Ontario. Caitlin, there has to be a clue here."

"Why?"

Dani ignored the question. "Problem is, there doesn't seem to be anyone else here." She led the perspiring pair to a graveyard at the back of the church. Great limbs of white pine creaked over crooked gravestones with faded names and dates. The girls felt a shiver despite the heat.

But the sight of the graveyard didn't inspire fear nearly as much as did the voice from over their shoulder.

"Didn't mean to scare ya," a tall, thin man said, barely opening his mouth to keep his cigarette from falling out. The man leaned on a rake and studied the girls, peering out from behind a decrepit headstone. He seemed relieved to find a distraction from his chores.

When some air returned to her lungs, Dani spoke in a shaky voice. "It's just that we weren't expecting… 'Cause we're looking, that is, we need to speak to—"

"Name's Razor O'Rourke. What can I do ya for?"

For once Dani seemed unable to speak.

"It's a long story, mister," Caitlin said with a sigh, "and we really don't want to take much of your time."

"Heck, I got all the time in the world, just like them," Razor said, flicking ash in the direction of the headstones.

Dani recovered her voice and began slowly. "Yes, well, um, do you know Armand Deschamps?"

Razor scratched the razorless bristle on his chin. "Yeah, sure. Used to, anyways."

"How long has it been since you had contact with Mr. Deschamps?" Dani asked.

"Ya mean how long since I last seen Armand?"

"Yes."

"Haven't seen him since he got that notion about getting rich from some notebook. Been a lot of years, truth be known."

The girls couldn't tell if Razor's furious scratching was from a deep itch or merely confusion about such a scheme.

"Do you mean the diary about Tom Thomson?"

"Suppose that's the fella."

The girls looked disappointed. Razor looked hurt. "Wish I could help ya. But what's the big deal, anyways?"

"It's just that the diary has important information about history, about people," Dani said.

"Oh, well, then, ya don't need Armand. He's a big dope, even if he was my best friend. You need to talk to Bernice Lehibou."

"Huh?"

"Yeah, she tells people what they need to know about things. Calls herself a seer." Looking around the graveyard, Razor half whispered, "But everyone else calls her a witch."

Dani felt the rough surface of an old headstone with one hand and her smooth lucky stone in her pocket with the other. "How does someone find Mrs. Lehibou?"

"Ya don't. She finds you. But only at night and only here."

"Here?"

"Yup, and you don't even have to tell her you'll be lookin' for her."

"But, but, but…"

"Ain't it the darnedest thing? You be here tonight and she'll come and answer yer questions. That's all I know. She's the real McCoy, but she kinda gives me the creeps. Least that's what they say."

"Who says?" Caitlin asked, nose wrinkling as if she were going to sneeze.

"They say."

"Who are *they*?" Caitlin persisted.

Razor dug into his ear with one finger as if the answer might lie somewhere within. "You know, I've always wondered who the heck *they* was."

As Razor puzzled, Dani rolled her eyes. “Caitlin, that’s not important to this investigation!”

Caitlin placed her hands on her hips. “People are always saying *they say*. I think it’s important to investigate who these people are. It may actually save some time in the future.”

Razor continued searching the depths of his ear. “Maybe there’s a They Say Society or something.” He extracted his finger from his ear and resumed raking the grass. “Must be an encyclopedia of stuff that they say. Have to ask Miss Lipsett at the library in town.”

Caitlin smiled and hummed.

“Come on, Caitlin,” Dani said, jamming her hands into her pockets.

“Thanks, Mr. O’Rourke,” Caitlin said. Then she leaned toward Razor and whispered, “*They* say putting your finger in your ear can make you go deaf.”

“*They do*! Wow, guess I won’t do that anymore.”

Caitlin grinned and skipped to catch up to Dani, who was intent upon their next destination. She glanced over her shoulders and waved to Razor O’Rourke, who leaned on the rake and jammed yet another finger in his ear. As Caitlin caught up to Dani, she said, “Eerie.”

Dani stopped in her tracks, blew out a gallon of air, and said, “Wait until we have to come back here tonight. That’ll be eerie.” Then she plunged her hands back into her overalls and hurtled forward.

Caitlin skipped along. “I ’ear ya.”

"Yes, Dad...sure, of course we will...yup. Okay, bye, Dad. Yup, me, too. Bye." Dani snapped the off button on the cellphone, exhaled, and wiped perspiration from her frazzled brow.

"Wow," Caitlin said, "that was close. What would we have done if your dad had said we couldn't stay overnight with Shannon at her cousin's in Huntsville?"

"I don't know. Didn't think that far ahead. I just thought about Tom needing to prove he was murdered after all these years."

They say *it was an accident*, Caitlin thought.

Dani held her chin in her hand and surveyed the graveyard. "Now, where do you think we should wait? Under the pine tree or in the middle of the graveyard?"

"Dani, it's not even going to get dark for a while. Besides, if Bernice the witch is for real, she'll find us. Let's just sit here and eat."

Earlier the girls had walked for a mile or so along Old Muskoka Road until they found a store. On a budget of $7.24 and with the limited selection at Orme's Gas 'n Stuff, the girls were destined and delighted to dine exclusively on junk food.

Now the girls munched among the gravestones as they watched the setting sun and discussed the finer points of the case. As the last streamers of brilliant orange light shifted through pine branches, a wind swept the graveyard and clouds rolled across the sky, blocking the remnants of the summer sunset. Darkness descended suddenly and thunder rumbled on the horizon, which Nikki took as his cue to start circling in search of the perfect nap position.

Caitlin gulped. "Dani, can you please turn the lights

back on?"

"Wow," Dani said, "let's go sit under that tree. I think it's going to rain."

The girls went over and leaned against the trunk of the ancient tree. Gigantic limbs swayed in the wind, creaking and groaning.

"Sounds like our dads trying to stretch before a run," Dani joked.

Lightning flashed, momentarily illuminating the graveyard.

"Dani, when we talked about how dumb it was for us to stay overnight in a graveyard waiting for a witch, did we consider the thunder, lightning, and rain?"

Dani looked up nervously through swaying branches into the blackened sky. "Well, Tom Thomson's been outside in all kinds of weather for about a million years, so I guess we can stand it for one night."

"But being a spirit, he doesn't get wet or feel cold," Caitlin reasoned. Menacing thunder followed, coming closer with each charge of lightning. "Or feel thunder and lightning."

Pine needles swirled around the girls in little tornadoes. The two huddled together as the temperature and air pressure dropped dramatically. Hearts pounding, they waited for the next round of lightning and thunder, each time brighter, louder, and more threatening.

The next boom shattered directly overhead, and the girls cried out, but not from the deafening thunder. In the next instant a flash of light revealed a solitary figure standing with arms outstretched in the middle of the graveyard. The girls held their breath and waited for the lightning to come again. Laughter pierced the wind and again a flash of light exposed a human face pointed skyward into the eye of the storm.

"B-B-Bernice," Dani stammered.

"The witch!" Caitlin cried, her high-pitched voice straining like a sour note on a violin. "Maybe they have gelato at Gas 'n Stuff, Dani!" she yelled, but the words were lost in the wind.

"Come on," Dani said, rising.

"To the witch?" Caitlin almost shrieked.

"Caitlin, that's why we're here."

"Oh, yeah," Caitlin reluctantly agreed, thinking *dumb, dumb, dumb*.

Slowly the girls inched forward as one. Dani held her lucky oval stone in a death vise. Caitlin gripped Dani's overalls straps as if her life depended on it. Through the darkness they heard chanting—lively, laughing chanting. Something about "Spirit of the wind, mystery of the night!"

"What'll we say? What'll we do?" Caitlin asked as she shook Dani by her overalls straps.

"Dunno…dunno," Dani replied, her head bobbing.

Another shaft of lightning revealed Bernice Lehibou standing like a statue, smiling, eyes closed, breathing in the storm and the graveyard. And just as the wind mysteriously dropped off and lightning showed the woman again, she opened her eyes and looked straight at the amateur sleuths. "Isn't it invigorating, girls?"

Caitlin released Dani's overalls straps. "Yeah, kinda."

Dani rolled her eyes in the darkness to no one in particular. "Miss Lehibou?"

"Yes, child," came a throaty answer.

The girls edged closer. "Can we ask you some questions?"

Dani squeaked.

"That's why I'm here, child," the musical voice answered, steady and direct.

"Do…do…do…" Dani struggled. "Do you know where the diary about Tom Thomson is, Miss Lehibou?"

"Bernice, child." The next flash revealed a more subdued Bernice. Now she had her arms folded. "And your question is interesting, child." Again she thrust out her arms as if trying to embrace the storm, then laughed with sheer joy. "What else?"

"Well..." Dani struggled.

"Do you know who killed Tom Thomson?" Caitlin broke in.

"Ah, a question of substance. I can't answer you with words." A bit of wind swept pine needles and Razor's just-cut grass through the graveyard. "But listen and watch and you'll be given a sign—a clue, if you will."

When the wind rose furiously, Bernice shouted, "Watch, watch, watch now, child!"

As white light illuminated the graveyard, the girls gasped. A distinctive angular face appeared, framed in a gravestone directly in their path. A figure with hawklike features, a severe expression, and long dark hair seemed about to speak. As light passed, the image said something that was lost in the newly gusting wind. The girls strained to hear.

"Grey Owl!"

The girls clung to each other and again heard the words "Grey Owl!" Dani considered how to form her next question to Bernice. "How…what…why…?"

Frantically the girls waited for a streak of lightning to reveal Bernice so she could tell them what this strange apparition meant. But when the sky next exploded with light, the graveyard was empty, except for headstones, pine needles, and Razor's lone rake. Bernice was gone. The shadow of Grey Owl was gone. And the girls were left cold, dark, and alone in a mystery as deep and wide as a peal of thunder.

17
A Seeing-Eye Friend

Dani and Caitlin awakened surrounded by a much different graveyard than had shrouded them in darkness the night before. For most of the long evening that had finally and miraculously passed, the girls had lain awake under the great white pine at the north end of the graveyard, listening to strange noises and fearing phantom shapes. Now tree limbs swayed and whispered overhead, swishing across the crescent moon that had broken through dense clouds in the early morning.

The girls lifted themselves onto their elbows and squinted at the spot where Bernice had stood and Grey Owl's face had appeared. They were torn between disbelieving what they had seen and expecting the apparitions to return. Each girl was sure she hadn't slept a wink, but neither could remember when the blackness of night had given way to the light of morning.

Dani was the first to struggle into a sitting position, wipe the film from her eyes, and survey their grave situation. Framed in swirls of mist and grey light, the carefully landscaped grounds, courtesy of Razor O'Rourke, appeared innocent enough.

Caitlin slowly rose, spat out a braid, studied the grass and flowers, and thought it all looked pretty. She vaguely wondered why grey headstones couldn't have colourful floral patterns to cheer people up. Sinking back onto her cozy bed of pine needles, Caitlin pictured that serious Grey Owl fellow in bright pink and neon-green. She was giggling and beginning to dream again when Dani shook her awake. Caitlin opened one eye. "What's for breakfast?"

"Jos. Louis," Dani replied.

Caitlin thought about eating chocolate, sugar, and cream for breakfast. "Yum, the real Breakfast of Champions."

Dani looked at her watch. Ten seconds later she checked the time again.

"What time is it?" Caitlin asked, ripping open her Jos. Louis wrapper.

Dani glanced at her watch once more. "It's 8:45 a.m."

"You've got a really bad habit there, Dani."

Dani checked her watch yet again. "Right. We slept in."

Caitlin stretched. "Didn't sleep a wink."

Dani rolled her eyes. "We'd better start back soon. Remember, Shannon's going to pick us up on Main Street at 10:00."

"Do you think our dads will still be frantically running up and down Main Street looking for a running-shoe store?" Caitlin asked.

Dani's mind was on more serious matters. "Caitlin, this latest clue about Grey Owl is really tough to figure out."

"Yeah." Caitlin became thoughtful, too. "Hey, Dani, do you think Grey Owl would look good in bright pink and neon-green?"

"Huh?"

Caitlin frowned. "Of course, if he did wear those colours, I guess he couldn't keep the name Grey Owl."

"Caitlin! We're trying to solve the murder of Tom Thomson, 'cause his ghost expects us to, and save our friend Shannon so she can write her thesis with a new clue from a witch in a graveyard at midnight where we just happened to have slept last night, at least you did, with superconfusing clues from a guy named Grey Owl who's also probably a dead guy, and we don't know what the heck he expects and what we're doing." Dani folded her arms and waited for her friend's reply.

Caitlin looked hurt but said nothing.

Dani took a deep breath. "I think he'd look ridiculous in those colours."

"Me, too," Caitlin said. "Now let's go find out about this colourful Grey Owl character."

Dani plunged forward two strides ahead of her friend. "The way I see it, we have two choices. First, we check to see if the Huntsville library is open before Shannon picks us up. Or second...Caitlin? Caitlin?"

Caitlin was skipping along to keep within earshot of her friend. "Right, Sherlock. What was the third choice again?"

At 9:43 a.m. the girls and the ever-patient Nikki stood on Main Street, having determined that the Huntsville library

wouldn't be open until Shannon was due to arrive.

"Now for Plan B," Dani said, rubbing her lucky oval stone in her overalls pocket.

"Dani, why don't we just ask Shannon for some information about Grey Owl? She's supersmart. She's doing her thesis and she's going to be a doctor, you know. Still, it seems strange somehow that by studying Tom Thomson she can do brain surgery, but I'm only going into grade seven, so what do I know?"

"She said she specializes in history, so she must do operations the way they did them in the olden days," Dani corrected her friend.

"How did they do them in the olden days?" Caitlin asked.

"Well, instead of giving people drugs to go to sleep they told them to chew on a bullet," Dani said gravely.

"Yikes! With Shannon operating, maybe Tom Thomson is lucky to be a ghost," Caitlin said, deadly serious.

But further speculation about Shannon's qualifications were interrupted by the arrival of the Swinging Seniors tour bus. The girls watched as each occupant slowly filed down to street level until only one passenger remained. The bus driver took pains to guide this last passenger down the stairs as the congregation of Swinging Seniors eagerly awaited the grand exit.

"Now mind, I'd be all right on my own 'cept for the crazy stairs you've got on this rig."

Just as the girls were thinking the voice sounded familiar, a thin, weather-beaten face with intense blue eyes emerged from the bus.

"Sadie!" the girls cried out to the astonishment of the

Swinging Seniors.

"Eh? I know those voices." Sadie adjusted her glasses to keep them from falling off the end of her hawkish nose. "Caitlin? Dani? Tell me it isn't so."

"It's us," the girls replied, stepping toward Sadie so she could tell the difference between them and the Swinging Seniors crowding the street.

"Well, don't just stand there, girls. Give a body a helping hand so's this here driver can do something more important than hanging on to an old bag of bones."

The girls stepped up and each took hold of one of Sadie's bony arms as the driver protested that nothing could be more important than assisting the great matron. Earlier that summer the hundred-year-old Sadie had helped the girls with their first mystery and had proven to be a shrewd detective. Best of all, she didn't ask questions about what they were doing, unlike any other adult they'd ever met. As Sadie's feet touched pavement, the girls babbled. "How in the world…boy, are we glad to see you…how long are you travelling…how did you find us?"

"Now, girls, move over here away from the crowd and slow down or you'll start sounding like a pack of beagles. You girls talked about coming to Algonquin Park for the past month, and I didn't fancy staying cooped up with old fogies all summer in the home." The girls nodded and looked around at the much younger fogies, Sadie's new travelling companions.

"Least this bunch has a bit of life left in them," Sadie snorted, to the smiles of the Swinging Seniors.

Sadie continued with one hand cupped around her mouth in a conspiratorial manner. "But between you, me, and the beagle, there isn't much swinging going on. Why, not one of them even knows how to play a decent game of crib! Can you believe it? But I'm changing all that."

"We're really glad to see you," Caitlin said, "and we could use your advice again."

"We mean on a case," Dani explained.

"Oh, I see, this is business, is it? Well, then let's get started." Sadie rubbed her hands together with glee. "Don't get enough stuff to keep my noodle from going to mush in the *retirement home*." Sadie laughed. "Why, retirement's for the brain-dead, and I always admired that Sherlock Holmes fellow. Couldn't stand to sit still, bored to bits without a case. That's why he took those awful drugs, you know."

Sadie's animated features were accentuated by creasing skin and moist blue eyes. Sensing the girls were preoccupied, she peered into their eyes. "Best spit it out, dears." When the girls hesitated, searching for the right words, Sadie held up her arm like a magic wand. "Oh, yes, yes, I understand well enough that you can't tell me the whole story. No matter."

Dani grinned with relief. "Thanks, Sadie. We knew we could count on you. You see, the thing is we really haven't many, that is, any substantial, clues in this case, except for a really weird—"

"And scary clue," Caitlin cut in, "from a witch!"

"Well, that's what people from around here call her, but she actually calls herself a seer," Dani said.

Sadie's eyes focused on a fixed point beyond the human field of vision, deep within her memory. After a time, she said, "Yes, people always do seem to throw stones at something they don't readily understand, things they fear. Sad side of human nature, my dears. Don't mean the likes of you two fine gals have to accept it."

"She tells people stuff about themselves that turns out to be true," Caitlin said.

"Which makes her all the more threatening to some folks," Sadie concluded.

"And the clue she gave us was pretty scary," Dani said. "She said the words *Grey Owl* as the face of a strange-looking man appeared on a graveyard headstone. I guess it's sorta hard to believe."

Sadie didn't faint or laugh, but again became thoughtful. "Grey Owl. Very interesting. Very interesting indeed. Yes, of course I remember Grey Owl. It was quite a story some seventy years ago or so. Archie Belaney was his real name. He was an impostor, much as ever lived. But he did some good and didn't hurt anyone. He was born in Britain but came to Canada and masqueraded as a full-blooded Indian. Lived as one for most of his life, told some great stories about the outdoors, preached about keeping our rivers and forests clean. Took a Brit posing as an Indian to capture the Canadian imagination."

Dani's palm was glued to her chin. "Sadie, this is real interesting stuff to know, but I can't figure out how it helps our case."

"Did Grey Owl ever have anything to do with Tom Thomson?" Caitlin asked with customary candour.

"Well, your seer really has come up with a doozy. I can't think about a single thing to link Grey Owl and Tom Thomson except, of course, that they both lived for nature."

"I think we need to tell you more of our story," Dani said.

"Too late," Sadie replied, looking at her fellow swingers. "This stop's just for ten minutes. We're heading for the park to look for moose! But this is a fascinating case, girls."

"But, Sadie, what should we do about the seer's clue?" Caitlin asked.

"Believe it. Sounds too powerful and strange to be a great big fib. What you do and how you use it to solve your case, I don't know. But there's a real mystery about a face on a gravestone, deep and God-like, so don't doubt yourselves. Use your—"

"Intuition," Caitlin finished.

"Call it what you like. I call it a lot of common sense and a little faith. But pay attention and something will break to help you solve this case."

The girls grinned. "Thanks, Sadie."

"Don't mention it. Now you can help me back up this here escalator. Bus driver really does have better things to do than carry me around, you know."

"I thought he was going to ask you out on a date," Caitlin said with an impish grin.

Sadie gave a little high-pitched chuckle as she crested the first step. "Clever girl. Now use your cleverness to find out what this sign means. Can't think what Grey Owl and Tom Thomson had in common except maybe the most important thing of all. But only a person who can see the world as it really is could understand it."

The girls looked puzzled as they tried to steady Sadie and their nerves.

"They were kindred spirits," Sadie said as she mounted the final stair. And with a wave from her magic wand, she was gone.

18
Howl It All End?

Shannon and the girls thundered through Algonquin Park in her red Volkswagen Beetle. "So apparently our hero Armand Deschamps actually did approach the McMichael about buying a diary that he claimed would absolutely solve the murder of Tom Thomson."

Dani let loose a low whistle. "Wow, so he *did* claim it was murder."

"But to hear it from the present curator, he was laughed off the premises and never came back. So…"

"So?" Caitlin encouraged.

"So…" Shannon repeated.

"So?" Caitlin countered.

"So," Shannon said once again, releasing an exasperated breath of air, "I guess that leaves us exactly nowhere."

"Well, maybe not exactly nowhere," Dani said thoughtfully.

Shannon seemed truly depressed. "Really? Unless Tom

Thomson actually appears and reveals the murderer to us, I don't think we—"

"Have a ghost of a chance," Caitlin broke in, grinning at two despondent faces. "Of course, Tom Thomson wouldn't just appear to people, that is, living people, and tell them who the murderer is, or was. I mean, he'd give a clue maybe, but you couldn't expect him to tell you the name of the murderer. What fun would that be?"

Two disapproving scowls turned briefly toward the back seat. "Huh?"

Caitlin shrugged, and the faces turned back around.

Dani sighed. "The thing is, Shannon, me and Caitlin—"

"Caitlin and I," Shannon corrected, then nearly bit her tongue. "I'm sorry, Dani. I'll start to sound like Dustin Fairburn if I'm not careful."

"Right," Dani continued, "the thing is, Caitlin and *I* think or at least feel that maybe, just maybe, we aren't exactly nowhere."

"But how in the world?" Shannon asked.

"Don't know exactly," Dani answered.

"It's just a feeling," Caitlin added.

"Kind of like faith, right?" Shannon said in a low, hopeless voice.

"Yeah, kinda," Dani agreed.

"Look, Canoe Lake!" Caitlin exclaimed, pointing at a sign. "That must be a good sign!" Caitlin's optimistic voice belied thoughts of doubt. "Well, at least the sign was real nice," she added with a hint of desperation.

"Do you know her?" Dani asked.

"No, she was there when I bought the car," Shannon answered.

"Not a good sign," Dani said.

As Shannon parked the car and they all got out, she asked, "Are you two sure you don't need me to hang around until your dads get back from Huntsville?"

"Oh, no, we're fine by ourselves, really!" Dani protested with a little too much enthusiasm. "We're just going to read in our tent until they get back, aren't we, Caitlin?"

"Oh, sure," Caitlin said distractedly, "we'll be like a couple of lounging beagles."

"Well, I suppose that's okay if you're going to be in your tent. I'll see you later." Taking great big strides, Shannon hurried off toward her campsite.

"Wow!" Caitlin blurted out to Dani. "That was close. If Shannon saw our dads—who are supposed to be shopping for shoes in Hunsville—here at our campsite, she might have thought she'd seen two ghosts." As the two friends plunged into the forest, Caitlin asked, "Why did you tell Shannon we're getting somewhere when we're really nowhere?"

"I don't know," Dani replied, burying her chin in her palm. "Something about the way Bernice looked made me think she must know something real important."

"I thought she looked scary and the face of Grey Owl was even scarier. But the Canoe Lake sign wasn't even a bit scary."

Dani scowled. "Enough with the signs, Caitlin!"

As the girls approached their campsite, thoughts of Grey Owl and other important signs were quickly forgotten in swirls of chaotic commotion. Dani's dad was walking and talking, a sure sign of agitation.

"Stores closed, a boat regatta, and now Warden Willins

to contend with! Two whole days lost for absolutely silly reasons."

Caitlin's dad thumped and stomped beside him. "And here it's almost noon and we still don't own a running shoe between us. What else could go wrong?"

But no one heard his last words because of the noise from the Toyota Land Cruiser approaching the campsite. The truck veered hard left and right to avoid the gravel road's many potholes but managed to hit every one.

The girls looked at the truck, at Nikki, and at each other and realized it was too late to make a run for it. Warden Willins had arrived. For a large man, the park official exited the truck surprisingly fast. All eyes were riveted on Nikki and his swirling tail. The warden was taking long, determined strides. Fortunately his speedy approach was momentarily delayed by his habitual need to adjust his pants. With his belt pulled well over his bellybutton, the warden began to move toward his destination once again. Panic reigned supreme. But Caitlin spotted an empty cardboard box and, without hesitation, flipped it over and placed it on Nikki. Everyone waited for a howl from the bowels of the box. Instead they heard the warden cough, then say, "Excuse me, folks."

Silence reverberated as the group waited for Nikki to perform his beagle acoustics. The warden interpreted the lack of conversation as a sign of respect. He pulled at his pants and squinted one eye to show the seriousness of the situation. "I've heard talk, from reliable sources, that you people might be hiding an illegal dog, a hound at that." Clearly they were boxed in.

John's eyes widened as Nikki shuffled a few inches

under the box. But still the silence remained.

The warden looked into John's eyes and noted fear. "This bein' the case, you'll know that according to park regulations either the dog has to go or you do."

Silence continued, except for a low, slow, rhythmic beat—Nikki's wagging tail against the box.

"Oh, I git ya. If you don't answer ya can't incriminate yerselfs." The warden surveyed the campsite, unsure what to do next. He tugged at his pants, which were sliding around his belly again. "Well, well, you can't hide behind the law forever! If you won't admit to concealing a hound, then I'll have to…to…come back, that's all."

Not so gracefully, he pivoted and hurried back to his truck. Sighs of relief turned to gasps of fear as Nikki began walking like a turtle across the campsite. As the warden drove away, he vaguely wondered how he had made them all so doggone fearful. Still, he enjoyed the feeling as he bounced off a pothole on the right and then on the left. But Warden Willins's happiness was undermined when he heard a chorus of laughter. He tightened his grip on the steering wheel, then decided it was nervous laughter, and grinned.

19

Murder, Mayhem, and a Mandolin

The setting sun peeled distinct layers of orange, pink, and violet from the darkening sky. Shannon and the girls slowed in the task of setting up their campsites as an invisible hand wove shades into ever-changing kaleidoscopic patterns. The lake lay eerily still, with shadows of hanging birch trees perfectly reflected in the evening light. Occasionally the welcome silence and calm of the lake were broken by a distant, exquisite call from a loon. A strange cry, so unlike any other forest sound, and yet in perfect harmony with the location. A cry from nature speaking to the loneliness of the human heart.

"It's no wonder this was Tom Thomson's favourite camping spot," Shannon said. "It's so peaceful. It's hard to believe he was murdered on the lake that was so much a part of him."

"And near his best fishing spot, too," Caitlin added with a quick look at Dani.

"What did you say?" Shannon asked distractedly as she gazed contentedly at the unfolding sunset. Then she sighed. "I can feel his spirit here. Can't you, girls?"

The girls grinned at each other.

"Oh, I know you think I'm a hopeless romantic talking about spirits, but look at that sky and think about what Tom Thomson must have thought taking in a sunset like this, standing on this very spot. I just know there's more to this life than what we can see!"

"You can say that again."

Caitlin and Dani jumped at the voice behind them cutting through the evening tranquillity with the intensity of a runaway beagle after a park warden's sandwich. The girls spun toward each other, searching for the voice. Caitlin's camping bag became entangled with Dani's overalls straps, and as the panic-stricken girls attempted to become disentangled, they fell onto a bed of pine needles. Together Caitlin and Dani rose to discover Tom Thomson, who sat by the fireside strumming a tiny musical instrument. Tom's smile widened as he noticed the pine needles clinging to their dishevelled hair. Shannon, caught up in her reverie, continued watching the sunset from the shore of the lake.

"Guess I can cause a bit of a ruckus appearing out of the blue."

Dani spat out a pine needle with far more effort than was needed. "Shhh, Tom. Our friend Shannon will hear you."

"And she's kinda nosy—real interested about theories and stuff. So she'll need a whole lot of explaining," Caitlin said.

"Nope."

"Nope?" the girls repeated.

"Nope," Tom said again. "Listen." He started playing the little stringed instrument on his lap. With a cheerful smile he sang something about being a lumberjack on the Ottawa River.

Shannon suddenly pivoted and said to the girls, "I know it sounds silly, but when I'm in the city I really miss the absolute calm of a Canadian Shield lake in the summer. It speaks to me in a way the city, with all its distracting noises, never can."

The girls' eyes shifted uneasily between Shannon and Tom, who continued singing and playing as if he didn't have a care in the world. Shannon's calm expression dissipated as she watched her speechless young friends. "What's wrong, girls? You look as if you've just seen a ghost."

Their mouths formed awkward grins. Caitlin giggled and said in a nervous, high-pitched voice, "And you look like you haven't."

Dani gritted her teeth, Shannon looked puzzled, and Tom finished his song and said, "Well, girls, aren't you going to introduce me to your friend?"

Caitlin glanced at Dani. "This is Shannon," she blurted, then giggled. "But, of course, you already know that, right, Dani?"

Perplexed, Shannon asked, "What's gotten into you girls?"

"Shannon's a nice name," Tom said playfully. "Is she interested in my mystery then?"

"Yeah, and she's convinced you really were murdered," Dani said.

But the girls had no time to puzzle, nor could Shannon interrogate them further.

"Murder. Who was murdered?" a voice demanded.

"I was!" Tom answered.

"Tom Thomson was!" Dani and Caitlin shouted.

"Ah, Miss Kennedy," Professor Dustin Fairburn said as he walked from his canoe toward the girls, "now you've convinced these two bright young people of your theory." The word *theory* flew out of his mouth as if he were spitting out a bug.

"I haven't convinced them of any such thing," Shannon answered icily. "They happen to believe, on their own, that Tom Thomson was murdered."

"Indeed. Based on what evidence? And who was this murderer? Was it Martin Blecher? They did fight, after all, the night before Tom disappeared. Martin was of Germanic origin. He and Tom argued about his sympathies for Germany the night before Tom drowned. As well, Blecher was something of an unsavoury character working as a private detective on occasion." The professor said the last words as if he had a bad taste in his mouth.

"No, no, no," Tom objected.

"No," Shannon said, "they argued about Germany and the First World War, but not enough to cause Martin to commit murder."

"Smart woman," Tom said.

"Oh," Fairburn continued, "perhaps it was Fraser, the innkeeper of Mowat Lodge on Canoe Lake. A man much concerned with money and petty things."

"No." Shannon said. "Tom and Fraser had a minor conflict over money, but not enough for murder."

"Hey, I like her," Tom said.

"So then the question arises," Fairburn said, "just who

might your suspect be?"

Silence.

"Perhaps," Fairburn began sternly, "your theory is based on speculation about a hunter or a poacher. Easy to propose, impossible to refute...but never possible to prove." Fairburn raised an eyebrow at Caitlin and Dani before continuing in a softer voice. "Surely, Miss Kennedy, as a scholar you have something factual, something new beyond ancient speculations. Well?"

"I'm not too partial to that fella," Tom said. "He's more interested in small facts than big truths."

Caitlin put her finger to her lips. "Shhh!"

"He's full of hot air." Tom shoved his pipe into his mouth and clenched it.

"You look like Nikki when he's seen a squirrel," Caitlin said, grinning at the artist.

"Shhh!" Dani hissed at Caitlin.

Tom's clenched teeth widened into a wry smile, and Caitlin giggled.

Shannon and Fairburn stopped talking and looked at the girls oddly. Then Fairburn continued. "Well, perhaps this isn't the time, or indeed the place, to debate this controversial matter."

"You can say that again," Tom asserted.

"I had planned to spend some time here in solitude in order to get a feel for Tom Thomson, the man, for my new book," Fairburn harrumphed.

"Well, I've got news for you, fella," Tom said. "I feel a lot different than you could ever imagine."

"Of course, I realize you don't agree with my academic endeavour, Miss Kennedy. You're compelled to chase some fanciful pipe dream, whereas I'm interested in resolving the real mystery of his accidental death by examining the pertinent question as to how an experienced woodsman and canoeist could accidentally die. Regrettably the truth is most fishermen die with their…that is…" Fairburn looked uneasy. "Well, with their flies down. In other words, they fall and hit their heads while engaged in performing basic human bodily functions."

"If I wasn't so bored, I'd laugh," Tom snorted. "This fella's actually claiming I peed myself to death!"

Fairburn fidgeted like a child in need of permission to leave the classroom. "I think I'll continue my canoe journey. Good evening to you all."

Shannon stamped her foot and folded her arms as the eminent professor guided his canoe across the glossy surface. "I'd give anything to be able to prove what I feel and show how wrong Professor Fairburn is in the process. I've read everything ever written about Tom Thomson's death, and the known facts aren't conclusive in the least. I just know he was murdered. Some things can only be revealed by following your—"

"Intuition," Caitlin, Dani, Tom, and Shannon all said in the same instant.

As the laughter subsided, Tom suddenly turned serious. "Follow your intuition, girls. It'll take you where you want to go, to what you need to know. It always served me well. I never would have made a single brushstroke without it. And it might just lead you to solve this old, so-called mystery once and for all."

20
A Case of the Pits

"Caitlin, it's time to get serious," Dani bellowed, striding ahead of her friend.

"You mean desperate!" Caitlin said, skipping and hopping along in tow. "I still can't believe Shannon got kicked out of the university! And even though her voice sounded calm when she told us, I think she was crying."

"I detected tears, too. Watson. It's time to get serious."

The girls had risen early in the morning with the intention of ending their dads' torture and returning their running shoes. They had barely set out for their running-shoe tree when Shannon showed up and told them all was lost.

"Officially," she'd told them, "it's because of a technicality, but the real reason is Professor Fairburn has withdrawn his support. So let's forget about the silly Tom Thomson murder mystery, girls. It was all just a pipe dream, anyway, and not at all realistic."

The girls hadn't known what to say. Telling Shannon

about Bernice and Grey Owl might have seemed a bit far-fetched. Besides, they'd figured the last thing she needed was a strange clue that was probably useless. The girls hadn't been at all convinced when Shannon had tried to make it sound as if being sent packing was really the best thing that could happen, but they had nodded in agreement, anyway. Nikki had seemed to understand that sympathy was called for. He'd nuzzled his substantial snout into Shannon's hand, licking each finger.

Now the girls were back in the hunt. "So what are we looking for?" Caitlin asked with a hop, skip, and jump as she pulled up beside Dani.

"Well, we have to find out what Tom Thomson and Grey Owl had in common. Why they were kindred spirits, as Sadie said. I think she might have hit on something important."

"Well, we definitely know they're both spirits," Caitlin said.

"Thanks, Watson."

"You're welcome, Sherlock."

Dani continued to stride and puzzle. "Sadie said they both loved nature."

"Right. And we'll have to find out if Grey Owl was a painter. But who's going to help us find all this information? Shannon said she was going to leave Algonquin Park soon."

Dani jammed her hands into her overalls pockets. "She said she wouldn't leave without saying goodbye."

"We'll just have to convince her to stay, that we need her here."

"But how?"

The case hung in the balance as the girls came to the

spot where they had ceremoniously strung their dads' running shoes. The spruce tree looked strangely bare.

"They're gone!" Both girls covered their mouths, fearing the latest disaster to their dads' running plans.

"Who…?" Dani gasped.

Caitlin groaned. "All we need is another mystery."

"Only the Grinch would rob our Christmas tree," Dani reasoned.

Caitlin sighed. "And it's only August."

Dani rubbed her chin. "Maybe this isn't the right tree. Maybe we're in the wrong area." She began to back up, studying the spruce from a different angle.

Caitlin started backing up, too, and happily noticed Dani didn't move a stride ahead of her in reverse. Maybe they should walk backward more often.

But just as Caitlin had this pleasant thought, Dani moved backward very quickly indeed, fell through a carpet of branches, and tumbled into a deep pit. Caitlin and Nikki fell just as rapidly.

"Dani, you okay?" Caitlin asked, lying on her back and looking skyward through broken branches.

Dani spat out a piece of straw. "Yeah, you?"

"Yeah," Caitlin said, sitting up.

Dani looked at her dog. "Nikki, are you okay?"

After an initial yelp, the beagle demonstrated complete recovery by sniffing out their new digs.

"What the heck are we in, anyway?" Caitlin asked.

Dani stood and stretched her arms upward. "Caitlin, I don't think we can get out of here. Someone has actually dug this pit as a trap!"

Caitlin relaxed on a cushion of straw. "At least it's cozy."

"Caitlin! This is serious."

"Maybe we can scream for help."

"But we're in the middle of the forest. Nobody would hear us."

This fact preoccupied Caitlin's mind for a moment. *Okay, so if we scream and nobody hears it, did it really happen? Of course, we'd hear, so I guess that answers that.* Caitlin decided Dani wouldn't be interested in this strange thought. "Maybe we could try lifting each other or something." Even in the dark pit Caitlin thought she could see Dani's face scrunched up in puzzled mode.

"It might be worth a try. Caitlin, get up and stand on my shoulders."

As Caitlin scampered onto Dani's back toward the summit, she began to speculate. "Dani, you don't think that maybe our dads found their running shoes and then dug the pit to trap us and punish us, do you?"

"Ouch! Caitlin take your running shoes off!"

Caitlin skipped down, ripped off her shoes, and started the ascent once again.

"Ouch, Caitlin, I don't think, ouch..."

"Dani, we're in luck. I've got hold of a tree trunk. I just need to get up another inch."

Caitlin was finally able to pull herself up enough to get her elbows onto solid ground. With one knee over the edge she'd be home free. But when she glanced up at the tree trunk she was holding, she was astonished to see a pant leg and a New Balance running shoe. The shock caused her to tumble into the pit again, landing right on top of Dani.

"Get off me, Caitlin. What the heck happened?"

"I…I…he…he…"

"Who? who? who?" Dani asked beneath Caitlin. But both girls became speechless and gasped as a shadow enclosed the pit.

We're too young to die, especially Nikki, Dani thought. *If we aren't home for supper, our dads will kill us.*

Then, to the girls' surprise, a soft voice whispered down to them like a welcome summer sprinkle on a hot day. "Hello. Hope you didn't hurt yourselves. I put lots of straw down there to make sure the fall would be gentle and cozy."

"Mr. Longfellow!" Dani said.

"I told you it was cozy," Caitlin said, fully recovered from her moment of speechlessness.

"Caitlin, it's cozy for you 'cause you're on top of me. Get off!"

"Oh, yeah, sorry."

"I think perhaps this time I could better assist you by pulling each of you up."

Within minutes the girls, Longfellow, and Nikki were sitting on the pine needles beside the pit, chatting like old friends at recess.

Longfellow's small eyes blinked furiously. "I had to dig this pit, otherwise they'd come and take me away."

"Mr. Longfellow," Dani said evenly, "only Caitlin and me—"

"I believe that should be—"

"Only Caitlin and *I* know where you are in Algonquin Park."

"Ah," Longfellow said, raising an objecting finger, "that's precisely what *they* would have you believe."

"Mr. Longfellow, who are the *they* people, anyway?" Caitlin asked, trying to solve her own little mystery.

Longfellow was pleased with the question. "That's exactly what I ask myself every day."

Caitlin grinned. "*They say* nobody really knows for sure."

Longfellow considered this for a moment. "Do they really? Very interesting."

Dani rolled her eyes in a great arch, taking in shades of dense green and pale blue. "Mr. Longfellow, Caitlin—" she nodded at each for emphasis "—we still have a case we're working on." Having caught their attention, she was at a loss as to how to proceed. Sighing with frustration, she added, "And the truth is we haven't really gotten far."

"*They say* detective work is very interesting," Longfellow said, trying to be helpful.

"They're right, except sometimes it does get boring," Caitlin contributed with her best bored expression.

"Mr. Longfellow, we never did find Armand Deschamps, and nobody we talked to has any idea where he or the diary is."

Longfellow thought for a moment.

Why did we ever think this nice, crazy man could give us a good clue? Caitlin wondered.

"Oh, Armand," Longfellow said distractedly, "I saw him yesterday. Said he had something important to talk to me about. That is, until he fell into the pit."

The girls' faces registered shock.

"Yes, that's about what he looked like, too." Longfellow grinned. "Would you happen to have any more of that delicious chocolate?"

21
When the Shoe Falls

Dani's fingers trembled as she fetched her squished chocolate bar from her overalls pocket. Longfellow's grin never left his chocolate-stained face as he manoeuvred the sticky substance from the wrapper into his mouth.

"Mr. Longfellow, are you just kidding about Deschamps 'cause we're kids or something?" Dani asked.

Longfellow carefully sucked the ruins of melted chocolate from each of his fingers. "Oh, no, I wouldn't do that. You two are my friends—my only friends. It's adults I don't like." Looking left and then right, he leaned forward and whispered, "Sometimes I fib to adults." Straightening, he declared, "I wouldn't lie to you two. Really, I swear."

As Dani scrunched her face to formulate the next question, Caitlin said, "*They say* it's not a good idea to lie to kids."

"Yes, I believe *they* do that," Longfellow agreed. "Yes, indeed."

Dani darted an impatient look at Caitlin, then returned

her attention to the hermit. "This is very important, Mr. Longfellow. If you've told us a little white lie, then we wouldn't blame you, but—"

"I assure you I'm telling the truth. Armand said he'll be here again tomorrow."

"When?"

"Well, that's a good question. I tend not to worry about time since I left the gallery, so I really can't say for sure. Sometime in the morning, I'd guess."

Dani let go of her overalls straps, settled back, and began to ponder her strategy. But Caitlin's next question interrupted her thought processes. "Mr. Longfellow, where did you get those new running shoes?"

Three pairs of eyes became riveted on Longfellow's feet. "They're quite nice, aren't they?" he said. "Bit of a squish at the toe, but you can't complain about a Christmas present in the summer."

Dani gulped. "Christmas present?"

"Oh, yes. My old boots were worn out, and it was no picnic to walk in them, I assure you. But *they say* you shouldn't ask too many questions when fortune knocks. These magnificent specimens appeared hanging from a Christmas tree. I didn't get a single Christmas present last year. This miracle almost restores my belief in justice, human dignity, and the possibility for lasting world peace. And the best part is there were not one, not two, but four pairs of almost-new shoes."

"Oh, boy," Caitlin said.

"Oh, no," Dani said.

Longfellow blinked, obviously confused by the girls' lack of enthusiasm. "You don't believe in miracles, do you?" He shook his long head slowly. "So young to be disbelievers. *They say* the youth of today—"

Dani placed her hands palm up on her lap, pleading her case. "Mr. Longfellow, the thing is, we do believe in miracles, but it's just that this time the miracle's not so much a miracle as it is, sort of, well..."

"Us," Caitlin finished.

Longfellow gazed from Caitlin to Dani, from Dani to Caitlin. The girls steadied themselves for profound disappointment, but instead a wide smile spread across the old man's face.

"Yes, of course, the chocolate, the shoes, it all makes sense, my little guardian angels. A miracle indeed. Bless you."

Both girls protested. "No, we didn't mean to...big mistake...only borrowed from our dads...a little joke...but, of course, we have to return the shoes..."

Longfellow glanced at the girls, his face blank. "I don't understand. You left a gift for me in the forest, near my home, a deliberate act of kindness, the one thing I needed, and now you want to take them back?"

"Oh, boy," Dani said.

"Oh, no," Caitlin said. "I'm sure we can find you some other nice shoes—and chocolate."

"And chocolate," Dani echoed. "It's just that these four pairs of running shoes belong to our dads."

"And they're sort of obsessed with...running in their shoes," Caitlin tried to finish.

"So you want me to give the shoes, your Christmas gift, back now that I've begun to believe in humanity again?"

A couple gazillion possible answers swirled through

Dani's frantic mind until one solitary, unavoidable response lay before her, naked in its simplicity. "Yes."

The girls felt terrible casting this cruel answer at the despondent, trusting old man. And the girls were shocked when the old man hurled back a well-played volley. "No."

"What?"

Longfellow wagged his long, sloping nose at the girls. "Finders keepers."

"But, but, but…"

"Unless, of course, you're more interested in getting the running shoes back than meeting Armand Deschamps." Longfellow's small eyes glowed when he was finished. "That's right, my dear guardian angels. If I don't get to keep these lovely shoes, you don't get to meet the lovely Armand Deschamps."

The girls stewed, not wanting to choose between an uncertain opportunity to meet the mysterious Deschamps and a fate worse than death should they not be able to return their dads' running shoes.

Longfellow became reflective and touched a long, deliberate finger to his nose. "Oh, and did I mention Armand said he was going to bring his diary with him—you know, the one about Tom Thomson?"

22
If the Shoe Fits

The girls surveyed the campsite from the edge of the forest.

"The coast is clear," Caitlin announced. "No Warden Willins and no sign of our dads."

"Right, okay, here's the plan," Dani said, pulling Nikki by the leash, ahead of her friend. "I'll hide Nikki in our tent, and you can put the running shoes back."

"Then what?" Caitlin said, hopping along behind Dani.

Struck by the question, Dani suddenly stopped, causing Caitlin to crash into her on the next hop. "Well, I guess we hope our dads will be glad to get one pair of running shoes back each and won't miss the two pairs we bribed Mr. Longfellow with to let us meet Armand Deschamps."

"Fat chance our dads will be glad we used their running shoes to bribe a crazy guy into letting us meet an angry guy who probably doesn't even exist," Caitlin said with a hop and a skip, putting a chink in Dani's armour.

Dani groaned. "We had to take the chance. This may be

the only opportunity we get to solve this case. Besides, we'll buy our dads some new running shoes later."

"How? We don't have any money."

"I haven't figured that out yet," Dani mumbled, unzipping their tent and letting Nikki pass out of sight and out of mind.

Caitlin carefully placed running shoes on their dads' pillows, ready for action. The girls then stood in the middle of the campsite, Caitlin chewing her braid and Dani holding her chin.

"Where the beagle is everyone?" Caitlin asked.

Just as Dani was about to answer, their dads approached the campsite, holding paddles and wearing life jackets.

"I think I'll master the J stroke by the end of the week," John boasted.

"I'm feeling comfortable in the stern," Bob bragged.

"We'll both be regular Tom Thomsons in the canoe soon," John commented.

"Oh, hi, girls," Bob said, waving.

"We just had quite a canoe adventure," John said chirpily.

"Maybe we can take you girls out canoeing after supper," Bob offered.

The girls stared down at their dads' feet, each wearing Peter Pan–like water shoes.

"Dad, your shoes!" Dani cried.

"Great, aren't they? Best thing in the canoe and very comfortable. Just glad the thief didn't take these, too."

"Not running again today, Dad?" Caitlin asked sheepishly.

"Nah," Bob replied. "We thought we might go into town to buy shoes after a short canoe trip, but we were having so much fun we decided—what the heck, running can wait."

Running can wait passed silently across the girls' lips, words never spoken by either of the skinny dads before.

"So what do you say, girls—canoe into the sunset after supper?" John asked as he and Bob walked over to their tents.

As the girls pondered the mystery of their dads' transformation, Warden Willins appeared from behind a clump of bushes. The warden's shirt was soaked with sweat and his chest heaved with obvious exertion. Perspiration dripped from his nose, and in a complicated, well-practised gesture he wiped his sleeve across his face while rescuing his sinking pants from below his waist. As he opened his mouth to speak, two loud, boyish whoops erupted from inside the tents. In an instant both dads reappeared outside, proudly holding pairs of running shoes. The men seemed to settle down a bit when they saw the soggy warden, but then John strode boldly forward and grabbed the park official's reluctant hand.

"Well, Warden, I can't thank you enough. I don't know how you managed to get them back, but I've got to give you credit."

Bob seized the warden's limp, moist hand as soon as he extracted it from John's enthusiastic grip. "And putting them on our pillows was a nice touch."

John's face scrunched up in thought. "Just how the devil did you figure it all out? It was that hermit, wasn't it?"

Warden Willins had had enough pandering from city folk trying to keep him from remembering why he was there. He was no fool. "Now listen up, would ya? I'm here for one reason and one reason only. I'm here to prove you people are harbourin' an illegal hound somewhere in this vicinity. No dog, specially a hound, has ever been able to ignore the sound of this high-pitched whistle."

As the warden made this declaration, he half smiled and pulled a sweaty dog whistle from his damp shirt pocket. Without waiting for a reaction, he blew until his cheeks swelled. The harder he blew, the lower his pants slid. Everyone stood transfixed until the warden filled his lungs and blew again. Once more the silence droned as the girls waited nervously for Nikki's first earth-shattering howl. The warden blew several more times until, breathless and frustrated, he had to steady himself against the nearest tree.

Caitlin and Dani held their breaths in expectation. Still no one spoke and, more to the point, no dog howled. For in the girls' tent, burrowed under cool pillows and sleeping bags, lay a very sleepy beagle. And although his ears twitched and his brain registered activity, the pull to beagle dreamland was too strong.

John felt he should say something, anything, and turned to Bob for encouragement. Bob merely shrugged and hoped Willins wouldn't have a heart attack.

The warden straightened slowly and prepared to speak but couldn't think of anything to say. Finally he thrust the whistle back into his soggy pocket, puffed up his cheeks, and stormed back into the bush.

John lamely attempted to conciliate with the retreating figure. "We appreciate getting the shoes back, Warden. We really do."

The girls smiled at each other. "Come on, Watson," Dani whispered, striding away, "we have work to do."

"Okay, Sherlock," Caitlin said, hopping and skipping behind her friend, "but I think our work is starting to show excellent results."

23

Just When You Least Except It

"So what do we do if Mr. Deschamps doesn't show up this morning?" Caitlin asked, walking easily behind Dani, whose pace was slowed by Nikki's many sniffing diversions. The girls had eaten breakfast, left a note for their dads, and set out from the campsite by 7:00 a.m.

"Well," Dani said, munching on a Fruit Roll-Up, "we go to Plan B."

"And what's Plan B?" Caitlin asked, bumping into her friend as Nikki took exception to the movement of a red squirrel.

"Plan B is where we discuss what to do next if Mr. Deschamps doesn't show up this morning."

"That's a good plan," Caitlin said cheerfully.

Nikki howled at the sight of Longfellow rising from under his pine-bough hideaway. "Good morning, my young travellers," the old man said, standing and swaying like a craggy pine but dressed in old flannel, faded tweed, and new running shoes.

"Good morning!" the girls replied without looking at the living pine boughs where Longfellow's face was located. Instead they spoke to the shoes before turning their attention upward.

Longfellow placed a long finger on his temple and said in a pleasant voice, "They're rather nice, aren't they?"

"Oh, sure," Dani said.

"But they look kinda tight in the toes," Caitlin said.

"Yes, yes, indeed they are," Longfellow agreed. "But they're a dream compared to what I used to wear. Here, let me show you." With these words he disappeared back into his hideaway.

"Caitlin," Dani whispered, "why did you say that? Now we have to look at his smelly old boots."

"He told us last time they were kinda tight, and I thought maybe we could talk him into trading for a bigger pair."

Dani thought about this. "Not bad thinking, actually, even if it did backfire."

Longfellow reappeared, gingerly carrying two enormous and decrepit boots. Carefully he set the boots on a log for inspection, then sat beside them and motioned for the girls to sit at the other end. A distinct odour of decay, mould, and stale socks mixed with a more tolerable smell of pine needles greeted the girls' nostrils.

As the unlikely trio sat like bumps on a log, Longfellow spoke. "Yes, of course, to you this is just trading old boots for new shoes, but to me it's much more significant—symbolic, really. The difference between prosperity and despair, abundance and scarcity, have and have-not—"

Dani coughed discreetly but with the intention of being heard.

"Life-affirming and life-defeating." Longfellow seemed to hear the echo of Dani's cough after a few seconds. "Um, yes, young one, do you wish to speak?"

"Yes, Mr. Longfellow. If you don't mind, that is, if it's not too much trouble, we were wondering about the arrival of Mr. Deschamps."

Longfellow's face went blank as if he didn't have a clue what Dani was talking about. "Armand here? Yes, yes, he did say he'd come, didn't he?"

Dani groaned. "Mr. Longfellow, you promised!"

"In exchange for the running shoes…hello," Caitlin said, mildly perturbed.

"Yes, yes, I did say that, so it must be true," the hermit agreed without conviction.

"When, Mr. Longfellow?" Caitlin pressed. "When did he say he'd come?"

"Oh, anytime now, I expect."

The girls became silent as they puzzled over these puzzling answers.

Longfellow continued. "Two winters. That's right, two winters with this heel flapping open." He held his boot on his lap and, as he opened the heel flap to reveal a sizable hole, a clump of mouldy paper fell out. "Why, it was so cold I had to insulate with this paper here. Didn't do much good, but in the cold of winter you'll try anything for a bit of relief." As he spoke, another fragment of faded paper fell out and drifted onto the pine needles in front of the girls. "I expect these new shoes will work just fine in winter with a pair of plastic bags over top."

Nikki suddenly became interested in the smell in the wild and pounced on the aromatic paper in Longfellow's shoes. Dani pulled the dog back on the leash and absent-mindedly asked, "What's this old paper from?"

Caitlin picked up a piece with one hand and held her nose with the other. Keeping the paper as far from her face as possible, she said, "It's in French."

"I've been saving plastic bags and elastics, too, because this winter I'm going to be ready." Longfellow paused as Dani's question reached his consciousness. "Paper?" A look of profound concentration passed over his face as he repeated the word.

"From the boot," Caitlin encouraged.

Dani tried to read the fragment of paper Caitlin held about a mile from her body. Then Dani lifted one of the boots and gently pulled the flap down. More clumps of the same yellowed paper tumbled out. Hopewell Avenue Public School's French immersion had never come in handier.

"Something about camp and loggers," Caitlin said. She reached into the top of each boot and discovered full pages folded in half.

Dani opened one bundle, and Caitlin unfolded the other. Each read quietly for a few minutes. Suddenly Dani's head rose and she sat bolt upright. "Oh, my gosh!"

At that precise moment Caitlin spat out her braid and cried, "Holy beagle!"

Both girls looked up at Longfellow, whose lips quivered as he struggled to say, "D-d-diary."

"Diary!" the girls repeated.

"Yes, that's right. Why, I'd forgotten all about that."

"All about what exactly?" Dani asked, carefully enunciating each word.

"Armand's diary, of course."

"Armand's diary!" the girls repeated.

Longfellow stood full-length among the pines, pulling long fingers across his long chin. "I'd forgotten what I'd done with that. Guess that's why Armand was upset with me back then. Now I feel silly about trapping him in the pit that time." The hermit sat back on the log and folded his long arms. "Guess I must have dreamed he said he was coming. Sorry, girls. But the running shoes..."

Dani's voice was firm *and* unsteady as she said, "Mr. Longfellow, sir, we aren't upset if Mr. Deschamps doesn't come if this is really his father's diary. But are you sure it's the diary that talks about Tom Thomson?"

Longfellow thought for a few moments. Seconds seemed like hours. The girls held their breath, suspended between wanting Longfellow to answer and wanting to read the decomposing composition in their hands.

"I thought I'd lost the diary, but I just put it to good use. Of course, with my new running shoes and a couple of plastic bags, I won't need it anymore. You aren't going to take them back, are you, since Armand isn't going to show up?"

"No, Mr. Longfellow," Caitlin said, "we won't take the running shoes back, but we really need to know if this is the diary about Tom Thomson!"

Longfellow grinned. "Oh, sure he's in there. Tell you what, you can have the diary if I can keep the running shoes, and we'll just forget about old Armand. Between us, he's a bit of a crank, anyway."

But the girls were already intently perusing the diary. The cover was long gone, as were some of the pages at the beginning and end. The amateur detectives worked quickly, shuffling through to try to fit the fragile diary into some kind of order. Luckily the entries were dated, and the handwriting, though sometimes faint, was neat and legible.

"Okay, Caitlin," Dani finally said, "we have from November 7, 1912, until March 30, 1918."

The girls read together, nodding at the end of each page. Caitlin chewed her braid furiously, thrilled by the task at hand. "Armand's father was the cook for a bunch of loggers, and he wrote this diary when he was in the bush."

"And they logged in Algonquin Park," Dani said with mounting excitement. "They worked for a fellow by the name of J. R. Booth, and then it says in English that he was a 'lumber baron.'"

"What's a baron?" Caitlin asked.

"It means he was part of the royal family," Dani replied, "just below being king, I think."

"Wow!"

Longfellow raised a long finger in objection, but neither girl noticed. Dani sat forward, intent on the page, chin in hand. "Sounds like it was hard work."

"He worked in a caboose shanty that had fifty-two loggers sleeping inside," Caitlin said.

"Wow!" Dani exclaimed without looking up.

"And he had to get up at four in the morning to begin cooking. And he says he was glad when the loggers were gone to chop trees 'cause they all smelled pretty bad." Caitlin held her nose, then, noticing what she was reading, held it tighter.

"But I don't see anything about Tom Thomson," Dani said with a knitted brow.

"Maybe we should flip through, look for his name, and read the other stuff later," Caitlin suggested.

"Right," Dani said.

"December 7, 1917," Longfellow said casually.

"But what if the stuff about Tom Thomson was on one of the pages...like this one," Caitlin said, holding a ruined strip with two fingers and pinching her nose with another two.

"December 7, 1917," Longfellow said again.

Dani exhaled. "I thought about that. A murder never solved, history never known because of a winter boot."

"December 7, 1917," the hermit repeated.

The girls looked at the old man. "Huh?"

"I said the diary tells about the murder of Tom Thomson on the page dated December 7, 1917."

Two jaws dropped as the third broke into a grin and asked, "Now how about some chocolate?"

24
Trailing Clouds of Glory

"Caitlin, pinch me," Shannon instructed from the stern of the canoe. Caitlin turned from her position on the thwart and pinched Shannon's thigh.

"I hope that helps," Caitlin said sincerely.

"Can this really be happening?" Shannon said, missing a stroke and almost tipping the canoe as she rubbed her bruised leg.

"Shannon?" Dani called from the bow.

"Yes, my detective friend?"

"If you tip the canoe and we drown, I don't think there'll be a diary around in eighty or so years to tell people what really happened."

"Sorry, girls." Shannon stopped paddling again. "It's just that I still can't believe these past few days."

"Same with our dads," Caitlin said.

"My dad's so excited he's miserable," Dani said.

Caitlin grinned. "You'd almost think people weren't

used to reporters and TV cameras when they go camping."

"It was kinda fun," Dani said.

"Until the CBC reporter asked me to comment on Dustin Fairburn's reaction," Shannon fumed.

Together the girls mimicked the defeated professor. "'Let's not get carried away with this so-called authentic diary. Let's consider second sober thought.'"

"But I would have loved to have seen Dustin's face when the curator of the McMichael Collection confirmed the diary's authenticity," Shannon said. Then she sighed. "And who knows? Since the president of the university has personally welcomed me back into the Ph.D. program, maybe Dustin and I will work together again. But, girls, I didn't like the way the reporters kept ignoring you and focusing on me. I couldn't convince them that you found the diary, not me. Did you tell them something I don't know about?"

Dani grinned and looked straight ahead. "Why would we do that?"

"You know adults," Caitlin said wistfully. "They never believe kids. Besides, it's better this way."

"But I don't understand," Shannon said. "How did you know Mr. Longfellow had the diary?"

"Intuition," both girls answered.

"Huh?" Shannon said.

Dani pointed. "There's Tom Thomson's campsite up ahead."

The canoe touched the shoreline as the dusk sky changed from pink to orange. After chaotic attention from camera crews, newspaper reporters, and foreign correspondents, the sounds of gently swishing pines and lapping water were welcome reliefs. Even Nikki was tired of howling for the cameras and was happy to settle back into his routine of snoozing for twenty-two or twenty-three hours each day.

After three exhausting days of talking about the diary and Tom Thomson's murder, the three friends set up camp in silence. Caitlin and Dani put up the tent and laid out their sleeping bags as Shannon made a fire. *That was quick*, Dani thought, looking at the steady flame. *Wonder why our dads couldn't do that.*

Shannon snuggled close to the fire with her sleeping bag and yawned. "I'm sorry, girls. I don't think I've slept a wink these past three days. Oh, I almost forgot to mention that Mr. Longfellow agreed to try the home in Huntsville. He said he could always go back to his hideaway if it doesn't work out. Dani, your suggestion was pure genius. He agreed to start treatment if he gets a chocolate bar every day. And, Caitlin, Mr. Longfellow said to tell you *they say* a chocolate bar a day keeps the doctor away." Shannon yawned again. "I really feel connected to this place somehow." She stared at the fire for a few minutes, mesmerized by the dancing flame, then drifted into a deep, restful slumber.

The girls watched Shannon sleep for a few moments. Then Caitlin waved her hands in front of the woman to make sure she wasn't faking.

"Okay, Sherlock, she's sleeping like a beagle."

"Good, 'cause with all the commotion going on we haven't had a minute to talk or even think about Tom."

Caitlin grinned. "Do you mean Tom Thomson or Tom Turkey?"

"Gobble, gobble, gobble."

Both girls fell off the log they had been sitting on and

turned their heads to gaze at the spectacle behind them. Strutting around the campsite with a pipe between his teeth was Tom Thomson, flapping his arms and sticking his head out in his best imitation of a turkey.

Caitlin laughed and Dani groaned. As the girls brushed themselves off and faced Tom, whose movements became more and more exaggerated, Dani joined Caitlin in laughing out loud. Having achieved the effect he wanted, Tom walked over to the girls and lit his pipe. With a twinkle in his eyes he blew out his match and said, "A job well done, girls."

Shannon moved restlessly in her sleep and the girls feared she would waken.

"She sleeps like an angel," Tom marvelled.

The girls glanced at each other knowingly. Shannon's calm face distorted for a moment as if pained by a bad memory. She whispered, "I know you're here… Tom…Tom, is that you?" Then she smiled, her face relaxed, and her breathing became slow and steady.

The painter continued to gaze at Shannon's face.

"Tom," Dani called.

"Tom," Caitlin echoed.

After a few moments, the artist managed to pull his eyes away from Shannon's slumbering face. "Sorry, girls, here you've solved this eighty-five-year-old murder and I'm just starin' at a pretty face. I never painted portraits, but with her face I might have tried. So, girls, the diary wasn't so hard to find, now was it?"

"Well, it wasn't exactly easy, either, Tom," Dani said.

"Oh, I know it wasn't easy. I meant to say it wasn't that difficult for two fine detectives like yourselves."

Caitlin beamed almost as much as her glowing friend.

"But, Tom," Dani said, "we're still not exactly sure why Billy Bull murdered you."

"And we kinda thought that somehow a fellow by the name of Grey Owl might be involved," Caitlin added, scrunching her nose. "But he wasn't mentioned in the diary."

"Oh, yes. Grey Owl was an important influence on me and my work. But accordin' to history, we never even met. Never could have, *they say*. I'll have to thank Bernice someday, even if you did find the diary and solve the murder without the Grey Owl connection."

Dani stroked her chin. "We kinda figured Bernice was trying to tell us that you and Grey Owl were kindred spirits and maybe 'cause of that Billy Bull murdered you."

"Is Bernice a witch?" Caitlin asked nervously.

Tom puffed on his pipe and smiled. "I wasn't always a good judge of character, but I sure got it right when I asked you two detectives to solve this crime. Bernice? Calls herself a seer, townsfolk call her a witch. Same thing, really. Truth is, she's one of those rare types who can connect the living world with those like me who must walk and canoe in spirit."

"She seemed lonely somehow," Caitlin said.

"Funny you should say that," Tom said, nodding. "Most people think people like Bernice are crazy, but they tend to be loners, for sure. Caught between two worlds, physically in the living world but belongin' more to the world of spirits. It's a gift, but the seer pays a price."

The last streaks of dark orange gave way to the deep purple of night as the sun imperceptibly slid below the horizon. The fire crackled and an owl let loose with his first nocturnal hoot.

"So she really did give a hoot," Caitlin joked.

Dani rolled her eyes without effect in the fading light.

Tom laughed. "Bernice is a good person, and like Grey Owl, she really does give a hoot."

"So you did meet Grey Owl?" Dani asked. "How did that happen? After that night with Bernice we heard some stuff about him. We know he loved the outdoors, just like you did."

"Yes, Grey Owl loved nature, but our connection, even if we only met once, was deeper that that. Here's what happened." Tom leaned forward on his elbows, sitting comfortably on a log. The girls moved toward the painter and the fire, not wanting to miss a word.

"History's a funny thing. People speculate about other people long after they're dead, long after there's any way of knowing what really happened, and then their version, their speculatin', becomes the truth. But you can't really get at the truth about something important with just a few facts."

"Huh?" both girls said.

"Sorry, girls, I get carried away sometimes. In 1912 I stayed most of the winter after that first summer in Algonquin Park. Went to Toronto in the late fall for a while, but I had this idea of painting trees, snow, lakes, wind, the works in winter. So I returned to Algonquin and sketched. But my sketches were all destroyed, which is another story.

"What matters is that on a Tuesday in December, Mark Robinson and I went for a long walk. Mark was a warden in the park and used to keep me company on some of my sketchin' outings. It was a frosty morning, the kind that covers everything. After freezin' rain and a warm spell, it turned real cold. Ice everywhere. The beauty was indescribable in words, so I painted it instead. I remember walkin' with Mark and turnin' to look at him 'cause he said something funny. His moustache was frozen like jewels, even if it was mostly snot. It was beautiful glistenin' in the sun—more spectacular than a priceless diamond to those who choose to really see. I remember feelin' that anything was possible and that something important was going to happen. That's when we saw him.

"He didn't call himself Grey Owl then, but he was dressed like him and he was in trouble. His moccasins were soaked 'cause he'd gone through the snow into a stream. He didn't want to take our offer of help at first—a warm fire and hot meal. The man was a real independent type, just like me, and I think he was feelin' a bit the fool for needin' a hand. But he was wet and getting cold, and eventually he agreed to come along to Mark's cabin. He stayed the night and talked my ear off. Said stuff I'd never heard before, never even considered about the park, the area, Canada. The beauty of God's canvas was being touched by a hand that didn't care. Progress.

"See those white pine trees?" Tom pointed at the trees towering overhead, and the girls nodded. "Time was, before the timber companies came, white pines two hundred and three hundred years old were everywhere in this park and across Canada. In Europe Canada was considered the land of pine—too many giant trees ever to worry about overlogging. But even in the winter of 1912 most of the biggest and oldest trees were gone. And the J. R. Booth Lumber Company planned to have 'em all."

"We read about the Booth Lumber Company," Dani said.

"Booth lived in Ottawa and owned the biggest lumber company in the world. Sure, there were some bigger companies, specially in the U.S., but Booth had the biggest owned by one person. At its peak he employed about five thousand men, and that's a fact." Tom jammed his pipe back in his mouth and folded his arms for effect, then continued.

"Grey Owl had only been in the park for two days, but he seemed to understand what was happenin', what the future would be. And he was right. Most of the great white pines are gone now. I became determined to accept Grey Owl's wisdom and take up his mission, even though I'd never heard of the word *conservation*. I talked to some people, wrote to some newspapers and government types over the years. Didn't easily express myself with words, at least at first, but Mark helped me some. Caused some commotion, and I'd have done a lot more, but my time ran out. Truth is, with the war on, nobody was much interested in a few trees. People didn't—wouldn't—understand. Didn't care.

"Then, on July 8, 1917, I got drunk and started talkin' with a bunch of fellas at Martin Blecher's place over there on the lake. I'd heard the lumber companies weren't too pleased with me, and apparently one government minister took notice and thought I had a point. What I didn't know was that the Booth Lumber Company had sent up a foreman named Billy Bull, a tough guy, to take care of the problem. I was the problem and I walked right into it. That night at the Blecher place I argued with Shannon Fraser about the money he owed me, and I argued with Blecher about the war. But the real trouble came 'cause I argued with Billy Bull about the future of the park. He called them lumber, I called them trees. And I admit I was frustrated about not being in the war, about a woman I once loved and another I didn't want to marry, and I tended to be a bit hot-tempered when I got into the liquor."

Tom stopped to calm himself. He stared into the darkness for a moment reconciling himself to the truth of distant memories before resuming his tale. "We had terrible words at Blecher's place, but the next day I couldn't have even told you what we'd said. Just past noon I set out to go fishin', still feelin' the effects of the alcohol and foolish about the night before. I wasn't payin' particular attention to anything. Wrapped my ankle, which I'd sprained, with fishin' line. Packed some lunch—still remember the bread and bacon. Then I slowly paddled across the lake."

The artist pointed through the darkness to the water's edge, his face a mask, his voice emotionless. "I didn't even notice his canoe coming at me. When I finally did look up, Billy Bull was no more than thirty feet away. Like I said, I felt foolish about the night before, so I just nodded and started to paddle past him. I didn't want any more arguments about the rights of lumbermen. But before I knew it, Billy swung the stern of his canoe close to me. I thought it was a mighty queer thing to do, but just when I was about to say something, he raised the paddle, looked me in the eye, and said, 'A paddle ain't a tree cause it's made from lumber.' I was too surprised to shield myself from the blow, and the paddle hit me square across the right temple. Wouldn't have killed me but, as you know, I drowned. Last thing I remember thinking, sinkin' on my back and gazin' up through the water at the sky was 'My God, so beautiful. Wish I could've painted it all.' "

Tom stopped talking. The fire had burned to embers. The campsite was dark. Silence had settled between the three companions. Tom fell to one knee and carefully placed wood on the fire.

Finally Dani spoke in a huskier voice than usual. "A lot of people thought that if it was murder, then Martin Blecher was guilty 'cause of the way you guys fought about the war."

"Ah, yes, Martin Blecher. No, he didn't strike me with the paddle, but he watched. I noticed him standing at his cottage door just moments before I saw Billy Bull. In fact, that's why I didn't notice Billy till he was close. Blecher watched Billy murder me. Not much different than doing it himself."

Dani whistled low and serious through the dark stillness.

"What happened to Billy Bull?" Caitlin asked.

Tom relit his pipe. "Billy was killed by a falling tree the next winter in the park. A timberman's error, and he never saw it coming."

The painter read the girls' thoughts as he added, "Didn't give me much satisfaction, but it did seem to be poetic, or maybe artistic, justice somehow. Felled by a tree in nature, buried in a box made with lumber. More important, lumbering continued and the rest of the great trees were soon cut and taken away."

Tom heard a sniffle in the darkness, then another. Slowly a smile crept across his lips. "Strange thing is, I might never have made as much of an impact with my painting if I hadn't died. Besides, if I'd had my way, I'd have fought in that foolish war and probably been killed in a trench somewhere in France. Had a bit of the death wish in me, I did. It's funny, but I'm feelin' good about things now that you two have let the world know I was murdered."

"Funny thing to feel good about," Dani said.

"Oh, joy, I'm murdered, after all," Caitlin deadpaned.

Again the silence grew between Tom and the girls. Then Caitlin spoke in an unsteady voice. "A friend of ours says the worst thing is to live—or be dead, I guess—with regret."

Tom smiled. "You have a wise friend. It's true. I floundered in a lake full of regret for many years. You see, you can't really be ready for your final peace until you lay down regret."

Caitlin and Dani thought about Tom's words.

Shannon rolled onto her side and said in a peaceful, dreaming voice, "Tom..."

But Tom wasn't finished. "I've quit regrettin' what happened in my life, but I'll only admit to you girls that at this minute I'm sort of regrettin' not being able to get to know Miss Shannon a whole lot better." He grinned and gazed at the woman shyly and with tenderness.

"We're pretty sure she feels the same way," Dani said. "Don't ask us how we know..."

"'Cause we happen to be seers when it comes to such things," Caitlin finished.

Tom and the girls laughed, the noise cutting through the darkness like the splash of a body plunging into open water.

"One thing I'm still wondering, Tom," Dani said. "Why couldn't you just tell us all this stuff before?"

Tom nodded, acknowledging the inevitable question. "That would have been a whole lot easier, but easier is seldom the best way. We aren't allowed to speak directly of such things. Besides, I needed the diary, physical proof to make believers of the world, and we can't seek help from the living unless they're believers, unless the experience will be useful in their lives."

The girls were satisfied with Tom's answer, though as the silence fell once more they felt some sadness.

Tom seemed to read their minds again. "This is a victory, girls, our victory, and I have you to thank. Don't feel bad for me. The hard part is past. It's time for my reward. I won't forget you, Caitlin and Dani..."

The girls struggled to say something, anything, to express what they were feeling. A log rolled over the fire's embers, extinguishing the flame Shannon had so expertly built. The girls strained to see where their friend Tom Thomson, one of Canada's greatest painters, had sat, but he was gone. Nothing but the low light of the embers remained.

"Tom?" Dani asked in a low voice.

"Tom?" Caitlin whispered.

"Goodbye, Tom," Dani said.

"Hope you enjoy your rest," Caitlin added.

The girls climbed into their sleeping bags. It was a beautiful clear night and there was no need to use their tent. They lay on their backs gazing at the stars.

Finally Dani spoke. "I heard a lot of the stars up there are so far away that by the time we see the light, millions of years have passed and the actual star has burned out."

"*They say* it's true," Caitlin said. "By the way, good work, Sherlock."

"Good work, Watson."

A star shot across the sky, with a brilliant trail of light so powerful the girls figured it might last forever.

"I guess nothing lasts forever," Dani said sombrely.

"Guess not," Caitlin answered. "But maybe that shooting star was Tom, you know, changing from being a wandering spirit to finding his resting place. Maybe it's okay if nothing lasts forever."

Dani liked this notion. "I think you're onto something, Watson. Maybe that's what we're supposed to learn, after all."

"Thank you, Sherlock."

Dani thought about things forever changing and felt some relief that math class, for instance, wouldn't last forever. She contemplated this for a long time as she studied the ever-changing brilliant sky. She meant to say good-night to Caitlin but fell asleep before she could.

Caitlin thought about Tom finally letting the world know the truth and then seeking his resting place in a blaze of light across the planet. She watched as the stars glittered, slightly brighter one moment, slightly diminished the next. Never the same pattern. She meant to say good-night to Dani but fell asleep before she could.

AGMV Marquis
MEMBER OF SCABRINI MEDIA
Quebec, Canada
2002